TWO BROTHERS ON ADULTHOOD EXPERI DIFFERENT FATES AS THEY STRUGGLE TO FIND THEIR WAY IN THE WORLD.

The Sherbrooke Brothers is a powerful coming-of-age story that blends elements of gothic fiction and contemporary literature. Delivering parallel storylines, the narrative portrays the life-changing experiences of seventeen-year-old Alex and his older brother Rob as they embark upon separate journeys. Both young men face challenges that stretch their inner strength and mental resolve to breaking point. Ultimately, they meet radically different fates, demonstrating the power of choice to shape individual destiny.

"*The Sherbrooke Brothers* is a unique and startling novella. How do the brothers work their way out of the devilish pact they find themselves in? Who will survive — and at what cost? A truly engrossing thriller. Go there, but you may never return."— *Professor Gary Crew.*

"Brotherhood, relationships and masculinity. *The Sherbrooke Brothers* is a moving and insightful read for anyone intrigued by the deep connections and bonds that can exist between humans." — *Dr Naomi Stekelenburg.*

i

THE SHERBROOKE BROTHERS

Eileen Herbert-Goodall

Moonshine Cove Publishing, LLC
Abbeville, South Carolina U.S.A.

This book is a work of fiction. Names, characters, places and incidents are products of the author's imagination or are used fictitiously. Any resemblance to actual events, locales or persons, living or dead, is entirely coincidental.

ISBN: 978 1 9151 078
Library of Congress PCN: 2017933089
Copyright 2016 by Eileen Herbert-Goodall

Cover design by Lisa Cutler; cover image by Nadya Lukic; illustrations by Aaron Pearson.

Other Works

'Anchorage' ~ Brilliant Flash Fiction, January, 2017
'Remember?' ~ The Oddville Press, Winter, 2017
'Waiting' ~ The Fredericksburg Literary and Art Review, Fall, 2016
'A Dead Texan' ~ The Paragon Journal, October, 2016
'Out of the Blue' ~ The Paragon Journal, April, 2016
'A Daughter's Letter' ~ Spelk Fiction, March 15, 2016
'End of the Road' ~ Brilliant Flash Fiction, January, 2016
'No Man's Land'~ Rollick Magazine, October, 2015
'Silver Lining' ~ The Art of Losing (International Anthology), September, 2015
'Chance' ~ Beyond the Axis (International Anthology), 2015
'Raven Medicine'~ TEXT Journal, April, 2015
'The Decision' ~ Flash Fiction Magazine, December, 2014
'Flight' ~ FewerThan500, December, 2014
'Kate: A Story' ~ FewerThan500, October, 2014
'Journey' ~ TEXT Journal, April, 2014

About the Author

Eileen Herbert-Goodall is a writer of fiction and non-fiction. She is Director of Field of Words, the online writing organisation dedicated to helping writers hone their craft. She holds a Doctorate of Creative Arts, which she earned at the University of the Sunshine Coast (USC), Queensland, Australia. She teaches high school students through the university's Creative Writing Excellence Program. She is presently working on another novella, as well as a collection of short stories.

Eileen's web address is
www.eileenherbertgoodall.com

Acknowledgement

I would like to thank my doctoral supervisors, Professor Gary Crew and Dr Ross Watkins from the University of the Sunshine Coast, Australia. The advice and guidance they offered while I drafted this manuscript proved to be invaluable.

A person often meets his destiny on the road he took to avoid it.

—*Jean de La Fontaine*

THE SHERBROOKE
BROTHERS

x

West

The downpour pummeled Cal's Ute. The service station's sign was a beacon slicing through the wet. He drew on a cigarette. 'Sure you want to do this?'

Rob looked out at a sheet of grey. 'Already said so, didn't I?'

'You seem on edge.'

'Nope, just bored.'

They'd stayed the night at Cal's and driven out of Sherbrooke before dawn, leaving a note in the kitchen for Cal's mum, Patricia. A few hours later, Rob had called his own mother and broken the news; she hadn't been impressed.

'We'll get moving as soon as this rain settles. You know what my eyes are like. I can't see too well this time of day. The weather doesn't help.'

'Yeah, I know.'

It was almost dark. They'd been driving for more than twelve hours. Another three on the road would get them to Talinga.

'A change will do us good,' Cal said. 'You worried about your mum?'

'No. Why?'

Cal opened the window and a ribbon of smoke seeped out. 'She must be stressed about Alex.'

'We'll only be gone a while.' Rob closed his eyes and listened as cars roared along the highway. 'I'm not sure Alex wants me around anyway.'

'What makes you say that?'

'He hardly speaks to me whenever I visit him in hospital. Might as well be a fly on the wall. It was the same last time he got sick.'

'He's dealing with stuff.' Cal flicked his lighter, watched the tongue of flame, then let it die.

The rain eased and mist rolled in so that the vehicle seemed to be moving through clouds.

'I can understand you not wanting to get your hopes up again, just in case,' Cal said.

'Is that a fact?'

'That's how it seems, but I could be wrong.'

'You could be.'

'Maybe you're not afraid of anything.'

'I never said that.' Rob chewed a fingernail.

'Seems like you're running away, that's all.'

'No, I just need to write this story and have it published — simple.'

Waiting around made Rob uptight. It seemed like he was always waiting for something: for his father to come back to earth, for his mother to get a grip, for his brother to be cured, for someone to notice his writing. The first three matters were beyond his control, but succeeding in his career was something he'd set his mind to. The story on Talinga was going to take him places.

'I wish you'd cut the superman crap.' Cal nudged his glasses up the bridge of his nose. 'You don't have to pretend everything's okay.'

'Thanks for the advice.'

Cal stubbed out his cigarette and slammed shut the ashtray.

'Truth is, nobody gives a damn about how the situation with Alex affects me.'

'It's not like he gets sick on purpose.'

'That doesn't make dealing with the fall-out any easier. Mum loses it and Dad — he checked out years ago.' Rob switched on the radio and music tumbled through the speakers. The word 'key' shimmered golden before his eyes, then dissipated in the smoky air. 'I want to forget about that stuff.'

Cal toyed with his lighter again.

'Would you stop.'

'What?'

'Flicking that thing.'

Cal dropped the lighter into his shirt pocket.

'I thought there was a drought out this way?' Rob said.

'Not anymore.'

The rain stopped; clouds peeled apart, revealing a three-quarter moon.

Rob had wanted to visit Talinga for months, but managed to keep a lid on his plans in order to land a scoop. With some tight writing and slick visuals, the story could score him a by-line in a high profile magazine. There was even a chance of snaring an international publication. Stories on the supernatural were hot property.

Built back in 1888, Talinga had supposedly been haunted since the original lady of the house, Vanessa Clark, and her employee (caretaker, gardener, driver), Albert Bowen, mysteriously disappeared around the turn of the nineteenth century. According to local legend, she and Albert were killed when their carriage slewed off a track and ditched into Patterson Creek. It was said the pair were secret lovers trying to run off together. No trace of their bodies or the wreckage was ever found. Some believed this version of events was a smoke screen and that Vanessa's husband, John Clark, had killed them in a fit of jealous rage.

Then there was the priest whose death was linked to the bell tower. Who knew what had happened there?

The Net's gossip mill claimed ghosts had driven everyone away from Talinga but, with a little research, Rob learnt the owners were travelling through Europe, stockpiling antiques. Brian and Kate McGregor had lived at Talinga for ten years and were the property's longest-standing owners since John Clark died over a hundred years earlier.

Rob had also called Talinga's caretaker, Kieran O'Brien, who agreed to let them stay at the homestead, but refused to surrender any significant information about the property over the phone.

'Looks like the weather's clearing.' Rob rubbed at the windscreen with a rag.

'Yep.' Cal started the engine, backed up, and hit the brakes before throwing the vehicle into first. The car swung onto the highway, wheels sliding. He glanced in the rear-vision mirror, then jumped lanes. 'Here's hoping we don't end up bogged in the middle of nowhere.'

'Might not be so bad. We could find ourselves a ghost or two — drowned cattlemen, vengeful bushrangers, lost explorers, massacres — the outback's full of tragic stories.'

'What about the homestead? You think it's haunted?'

Rob shrugged. 'The place has been awash with rumors of adultery, murder and madness for years. Got to be something in it.'

Cal grinned. 'Sounds like a bunch of camp-fire yarns.'

'Could be a whole lot more, too. Guess we're about to find out.'

'I've got to admit, it feels good to go with the flow.'

'That's what I've been saying. You need to loosen up.'

'I'm trying.' Cal kept his eyes on the road. 'You can see that, right?'

'Sure.'

A truck travelling in the opposite direction sped past and the Ute shuddered. Across the seat, Cal gripped the wheel, his hands large and strong. Rob remembered the night they'd met, how he'd literally seen stars after dropping acid.

Now, staring out his window, he watched as moonlit trees raced by.

Fear

In a way, death had a certain appeal — it would be definite, final — yet Alex feared it. His anxiety was amplified by the emptiness that threatened to engulf him. Since being admitted to Sherbrooke Hospital nine weeks earlier, loneliness had gnawed at his insides.

Tests had detected the reappearance of cancer. This was the second time in three-and-a-half years that Alex had battled the disease, although his doctor reassured him the situation was not full-blown. Malignant cells were restricted to a testis. Alex received localized radiotherapy, followed by chemotherapy. He'd lost his hair again, but there was no trace of the cancer. The tumor had been obliterated.

There would be no soft landings; he'd probably be left sterile. Depression was a real possibility.

Most people he knew were making decisions about the future, but Alex was tackling one day at a time. He had no real plans. Sometimes he imagined himself masterminding an ingenious method for saving the world's coral reefs, although the dream to study Marine Biology really belonged to his girlfriend, Kelly Faulkner. Alex had partly adopted it through a strange process of psychological osmosis. He also loved to draw. Other than that, he had no idea about what to do with his life.

Prayer helped him cope. His faith brought with it visions of an escape route, a tunnel of golden light, where Alex would somehow know where to go and what to do. He took comfort in the idea of a higher force steering his life, but lately his faith had waned. What sort of God let someone get so sick twice?

Alex was first treated for T-cell ALL, Acute Lymphoblastic Leukaemia, at the age of fourteen. It hadn't been the death sentence he'd anticipated. Having entered remission quickly, he was expected to make a full recovery and sent home with a pile of tablets. Alex toed the line — he took his med's, saw his GP for regular check-ups, watched his diet — but things didn't always go to plan. Henry Knowles, the paediatric oncologist seated beside Alex's bed, remained positive.

'Relapse is relatively common, Alex. It affects around a quarter of children and adolescents with ALL. Most relapses occur in the good risk category, your category.'

'That's because less of the high-risk kids survive. The numbers are skewed.'

'That doesn't mean you're going to die.'

Alex stared at the wall. 'What does it mean?'

'All going well, you're back on track and will enter remission once more.'

'For how long?'

'Tests have confirmed this was an extramedullar event.' The Doc leaned forward. 'I'm sure you understand what that means.'

Alex nodded. Keen to make sense of things early on, he'd spent hours searching the Net for relevant information. Consequently, he developed an impressive command of medical terminology, including an understanding of "extramedullar", or that which exists outside the inner portion of an organ.

The worst type of recurrence involved a bone marrow relapse within two years. In such cases, the odds of survival weren't good. And, if the cancer returned, the best case scenario was to experience an isolated non-marrow event restricted to the central nervous system, or a testis; his situation exactly. What Alex really wanted to know was how the leukaemia had gained a foot-hold in the first place. Was the molecular abnormality that triggered his cancer something he'd been born with, or a random error that occurred later? Was it fate, or simply bad luck? The Doc said it was most likely both. He believed a nonhereditary gene mutation combined with a "second hit" factor, such as an early childhood viral infection, probably kick-started the production of abnormal white cells inside Alex's marrow.

Alex stared at the sheet covering the lower half of his body. Having cancer was one thing, dissecting its recurrence in search of a silver lining was something else altogether. He wasn't sure he had the mental flexibility needed for such optimism.

'I understand your disappointment,' the Doc said, 'but things are looking up. We've finished treatment and you're well into consolidation. You'll be home by the end of the week.'

'I suppose I should be grateful.'

Narrowing his eyes, Dr Knowles seemed about to say something when his pager interrupted. The Doc stood, removed the device from his belt and scanned its screen. Light streamed through the window, striking his black hair.

Alex rubbed his bare scalp.

'I'll be back tomorrow.' Dr Knowles hitched the pager back into position. 'Chin up.'

'Sure.'

The Doc walked away. He was tall and lean, his movements fluid. He stopped in the doorway and glanced over his shoulder. 'How's Kelly these days?'

'She's fine.'

'Good. It's important to have someone your own age to talk with.'

'I know.'

'Is she aware you want to go away?'

'No.'

'What about your mother?'

Alex shook his head. 'I'll tell them both tomorrow.'

'Maybe I should speak to Edie first, give her some warning.'

'I'll handle it.'

'Tread carefully.'

'I will.'

The Doc left and Alex turned to the window. Mechanical cranes punctured the skyline, their long, metal limbs moving with robotic smoothness. Sheets of glass glittered with sunlight. He could see part of the river far below. An arterial life-line, it pumped its way through a jungle of concrete towards the sea. The colour of its water changed, depending on the time of day, or weather. Mostly, it was dark and mysterious-looking. What creatures lurked in its depths? Alex was sure he'd seen some likely contenders in his dreams, especially after having analgesics. The occupants of Alex's sleep were usually mutant arthropods with body segments sharp as blades, threatening claws, bulging eyes. A few were strikingly beautiful, fluorescent in colour, angular limbs twirling like intricate machine parts.

Once he'd even dreamt of stymphalians, those strange metal birds that had taunted Hercules. He'd sketched all the creatures, paying close attention to their mind-bending proportions, so that over the past few years his folio had taken a decidedly grotesque turn.

He listened to the ward's heartbeat; a telephone rang, laughter tumbled down the corridor, a steady electrical hum seeped through the walls.

His mind summoned a vision of Kelly — her eyes, the colour of sky and sea, they killed him. But she'd be heading to a university up north before long; it was best to cut the ties sooner rather than later.

Stars: A memory

Rays of light streamed down upon the university's sandstone walls, but otherwise the courtyard was dark. Faceless figures wandered through the crowd, or lingered in shadows, dancing, kissing. On the main stage half a dozen percussionists sat in a semi-circle, slapping their drums and shaking the night. Fire dancers leapt across the grass, hoisting burning sticks into the air.

Orange flames sliced through the darkness.

Standing opposite the stage, Rob leant against a wall, vibrations knocking inside his chest. He looked down and saw half the ground was covered in grass, the other with lines of yellow, blue and red. His vision blurred as the image seared itself onto his brain.

The acid was kicking in.

He closed his eyes, concentrating on his balance.

There was something sublime about the drums; their steady rhythm sharpened his senses. At any moment his spirit might leave his body and astral-travel out over the night. What would the nearby river look like from high above? He longed to fly.

A vast sea of bodies swirled before him. Thousands of first years littered the crowd; he could tell by all the togas. His gaze drifted back to the young man seated on a bench close by. He had shoulder-length hair and wore glasses. Rob moved away from the wall and it felt like he was space-walking. Good thing he'd only dropped half a tab.

The drums stopped.

Glancing down, he noticed the elongated shape of his hands. His fingertips tingled. The pungent smell of dope filled the air. Rob took a deep breath. In the wind trees shivered, whispering secrets. He listened, wanting to understand, but a wave of human voices drowned out the sound.

The bench seemed to shift as he sat down. He turned and saw the stranger looking. It was too dark to make out the colour of his eyes. Rob crossed his legs and stared at the fire dancers.

The man adjusted his glasses 'You study here?'

'Yeah.'

'What?'

A full moon resembling a golden eye observed them from the bottom of the sky. Rob's thoughts slid, blurred, snapped back on track. 'Pardon?'

'What do you study?

'Journalism.' Had the word come out right? Rob suppressed an urge to laugh.

'How about you?'

The man shook his head, lit a cigarette. 'I'm not a student.'

'What do you do?'

'Paint, mostly.'

Rob stared at the man's teeth, which were shiny little blocks. 'Really? What sort of stuff?'

'Houses.'

Rob watched the word tumble, beautiful and white, from the man's mouth. 'As in paintings of houses?'

Slipping his lighter into his jeans' pocket, the man brushed against Rob's arm. 'No, as in house walls. Inside and out.'

'Right.'

The drums started up again.

'I have a friend who studies here. I lost her about an hour ago.'

'Shame,' Rob said.

A smile tugged at the man's mouth.

'What's your name?'

'Cal Taylor.'

'I'm Rob McKenzie.'

'You having a good night?'

'So far.'

Cal dragged on his cigarette, opened his mouth, and blew a series of perfect smoke rings.

Rob turned to the fire dancers, watching streaks of gold swim through the air.

Someone howled like a dog.

'Want to take a walk, Cal?'

'Where to?'

'Someplace a little more quiet.'

The tip of Cal's cigarette glowed bright. 'I was thinking about heading home.'

'You were?'

'Yeah. Want a lift?'

Tilting his head, Rob took in the stars. 'I had some acid a couple of hours ago. You okay with that?'

Cal stood, dropped his cigarette and crushed it beneath his boot. 'You going to turn into a werewolf?'

'Never happened before.'

'An axe murderer?'

'Unlikely. Can hardly keep a straight face right now.'

Cal smiled. 'Then I'm okay with it.'

Rob got to his feet and started space-walking again.

'You all right?'

'Sure, just a little scattered.'

Cal led the way through the crowd. A man dressed as a jester squeezed past, heading the other way, and the bells on his hat set off an electrical storm inside Rob's brain.

Brightly coloured lines of yellow, green and red streaked his vision before forming star clusters. The stars spoke to one another as they trailed the jester, their words nonsensical. Rob blinked and the hallucination vanished.

The crowd jostled. Rob's head spun. Reaching out, he clutched Cal's shoulder.

Cal turned. 'How you doing?'

'A little dizzy.' Rob closed his eyes. 'I'll be fine.'

'Come on.' Cal took him by the arm. 'Almost there.'

Out in the open, they walked in silence. Cool air rushed into Rob's lungs. The multi-storey car park loomed on the corner ahead like a fallen satellite. He could have sworn the building was tilting sideways. 'Sorry. I'm good now.'

'That's okay. It was pretty crowded back there.'

Beneath the street lights, Rob got a good look at the man beside him. He had a thin face, slightly hooked nose, blue eyes.

Christ, he was beautiful.

They jumped in Cal's Ute, tore off down the freeway, tracking a network of overpasses and underground tunnels. Rob surrendered his self-control. He played Space Invaders with approaching traffic lights, laughed as a trio of tiny astronauts swung from the bumper-bar of the car in front, stuck his face into the breeze. Beside them the river glistened. A dog leg of house lights, comforting in their suburban familiarity, tracked the river's banks.

Rob spotted a group of orange orbs floating above the river. 'You see that?'

'What?'

He pointed out the window. 'Those things hovering around.'

Cal looked towards the river, then back at the road. 'I don't see anything.'

'But they're everywhere — lots of little spirits floating above the water.'

'No, it's just reflected light.'

Rob stared hard. The orbs flitted above the river's surface, then swarmed together, congealing into a single glowing mass that formed an effigy of his brother, Alex. Without warning, the figure burst into flames and the river bled with violent orange stains. Rob's heart froze, squeezed tight, then lurched back into its autonomic rhythm. What did it all mean? Probably nothing, just the circuits inside his brain over-heating. Closing his eyes, he slipped inside a psychedelic tunnel where nothing seemed to matter much at all.

Blue

From the doorway of the hospital's chill out
room, Alex could see Boots. The old man sat on
the couch, listening to a radio perched on the
coffee table nearby. Music floated through the air.
Alex stepped into the room and moved towards the
computer positioned on a desk near the window. He
waved to Boots, who lifted a hand and smiled without
recognition. No one paid much attention to the old
man, who mostly blended into the background.
When Alex asked Miss Jennings about Boots, she
said he'd appeared at the hospital one day without
explanation. The staff agreed to turn a blind eye
because the old man was clearly alone in the world.

Weeks ago Boots had explained his nickname.
Nearly a quarter of a century had passed, he said,
since he'd become lost while hiking through
bushland. When he was rescued seven days later, his
clothes were tattered, his skin peeling. Only his
boots escaped unscathed. The name stuck. He also
told Alex how his wife had died of a heart attack a
couple of years back. Alex sensed there were stories
Boots chose not to tell, things his mind fled from.

He clicked the desk-top's telephone icon and
logged into cyberspace. Around 7:00 a.m. every

second day, Alex met his friends in the chatroom, ZeroGravity. Having crossed paths in the hub six months earlier, they'd stayed in touch.

The computer hummed, its electronic tendrils anchoring him to Earth.

He glanced at Boots, who was leaning forward, apparently enraptured by the radio's broadcast. Finding a trail of messages, Alex launched into the exchange.

I've had some nasty encounters of late. Any players interested in the gory details? — Dog Star.

Alex stared at the screen. His two buddies referred to themselves as Dark Angel and Dr Seuss. Both claimed to be first year university students, but on-line identities were notoriously dubious; people could be whoever they wanted. For Alex, that was part of the attraction. His alter-ego soared through cyberspace with a confidence he never felt in real life. The rush was addictive. A response came through almost immediately.

Greetings troubled friend. Have the lovely nurses been administering trippy pain-killers again? —Dr Seuss.

I wish, but no, I was drug-free at the time. — Dog Star.

What did u c? — Dr Seuss.

The Grim Reaper. — Dog Star.

The cursor's vertical eye blinked. Where was Dark Angel? Alex enjoyed her comments, which often prodded his brain, making him think. He imagined her with black hair, pale skin, and kohl-rimmed eyes.

I take it this occurred in the middle of the night, when all such creatures of darkness typically appear? — Dr Seuss.

Yep, about 2 a.m. I woke 2 find him hovering above my bed, scythe raised. Not pleasant. — Dog Star.

What did he look like? — Dr Seuss.

Don't know. He was wearing a hooded robe that threw a shadow across his face. — Dog Star.

Maybe u were dreaming? — Dr Seuss.

Still could have been real, dreaming or not. — Dog Star.

Interesting concept. Truth is, I don't know much about Mr Grim, except that roots of his personification can be traced to the ancient Greeks (as with most things interesting, dark and complex). He probably made an even earlier appearance, but such facts seem 2 be missing from my sorry brain. I do know the Greeks called Death Thanatos. He was a beautiful winged boy who could often be out-witted. Maybe that's where the idea of cheating death came from? Doesn't sound much like the entity u saw, though. I'd love 2 know what Our Lady of Darkness thinks. Is she in the building? — Dr Seuss.

Alex was aware of the hospital's background noise: something hit the floor with a metallic clang, an emergency buzzer bleated, footsteps hurried down the corridor. He turned to see that Boots had fallen asleep.

He was ready to start typing, when a message appeared from Dark Angel.

The Grim Reaper may be chronically misunderstood. — Dark Angel.

How long have u been tuned in? — Dog Star.

A while, say around 65 breaths. — Dark Angel.

Of what riddles do u speak, fair maiden? — Dr Seuss.

The average human takes around 13 breaths/minute. U do the maths, Myth Boy. — Dark Angel.

Funny how we take such crucial business 4 granted. — Dr Seuss.

Speak 4 yourself. Around my haunt there's far 2 many machines breathing 4 people who don't even know they're alive. — Dog Star.

A thousand apologies. I tend to type before I think. Anyway, I fear our conversation has strayed from its original thread. I was quizzing Our Lady of Obscure Measurements about the darkest angel of all, Mr Grim. In what way do u think he's misunderstood? — Dr Seuss.

Alex sat back and watched things unfold. Tapping into other people's ideas about death helped him feel less alone.

Take that grisly AIDS ad from '87. It scared everyone witless, with death knocking down rows of people like bowling pins. But maybe he's not evil. He could be more of a guide waiting 2 help the newly dead find their way somewhere. — Dark Angel.

Maybe 2 hell. — Dog Star.

U don't buy into all that brimstone and punishment stuff, do u? — Dark Angel.

The keyboard clicked in the quiet.

When you've wondered if u'll be alive in a year's time, images of a terrifying red creature jabbing a pitchfork at tortured souls drowning in flames tend 2 seep into your psyche, especially when you're sleeping. Then again, could be the drugs. I've seen some crazy shit. — Dog Star.

Fear can trail us day and night, as Mr Carver so beautifully observed. — Dark Angel.

Thanks 4 the tip, Our Lady of Soulful Prose. I do so love your literary cues. — Dr Seuss.

Dear Dr, sometimes I can't help feeling you're taking the piss. — Dark Angel.

Not true. I take your comments seriously and long 2 decode your mysterious allusions. — Dr Seuss.

Now you're hitting on me? — Dark Angel.

Is that so wrong? Is there some sort of cyberspace etiquette that says it shouldn't be done? — Dr Seuss.

How should I know? I don't make the rules. — Dark Angel.

Maybe there are no rules? — Dr Seuss.

Of course there's rules. There's always rules. — Dark Angel.

Scrolling down the screen, Alex realized his friends were probably crushing on one another. Did they ever think of meeting in the real world?

Dark Angel threw a ball from left field.

U don't talk about your parents much, Dog Star. How are they coping? — Dark Angel.

Alex had been waiting for this subject to rear its head and chose his words carefully.

I'm not sure 'coping' is a word I'd use 2 describe my parents' emotional state. It's complicated. But what would I know? Lately my brain circuitry has been blowing fuses every which way. Maybe I'm just pissed with the world. — Dog Star.

He imagined binary codes sliding down local optical fibers, preparing to reconfigure themselves as a thread of black on white.

It happens. Here's some trivia...I used to be bullied at school. Whenever I was feeling down, I'd pick up my Brain Atlas and drop it on its spine (unfortunate, but necessary). Next, I'd read from whatever page that opened. I figured if jocks were going 2 pay out on me, then I'd get my own back by doing surgery on at least 1 of them somewhere down the track. Us geeks already rule the world:) — Dr Seuss.

Alex laughed.

That helps me feel a little more sane. And I'll try 2 forget about Mr. Grim for now. The power of positive thinking, right? — Dog Star.

He logged out. That was the beauty of virtual friendships; the connection could be terminated with the press of a button. Behind him, Boots sat with his head tilted back, a wet trail seeping from the corner of his mouth. Melancholy music emanated from the radio. Grabbing a tissue from a box on the desk,

Alex walked over to the old man, wiped his chin, then threw the tissue into a bin overflowing with plastic cups.

Outside in the empty corridor, Alex waded through a current of dread.

He entered his room, sat on the bed and stared at a picture of Jesus hanging on the wall. Nails pierced the man's flesh, flagging a vicious reminder that his prayers in the garden of Gethsemane had gone unanswered.

Leaning against the metal bed rail, Alex glanced down at his hospital gown. What of his own prayers?

Talinga

The clouds had peeled back, revealing a great tract of sky in which a sliver of moon dangled. Vegetation fell away as they followed the highway onto an open plain. Scattered trees shimmered silver.

'Feels like we're entering a different world,' Cal said.

'Maybe we are.'

'You really think we might find something? A ghost maybe?'

Rob shrugged and stared through the windscreen. 'Sure feels weird out here. Like we're closer to space.'

'Yeah. I've never seen stars so bright.'

The homestead stood in the distance, its windows glowing yellow. As they drew near, their headlights revealed a single-storey building, rectangular in shape with sweeping verandas.

Cal parked beside a white Cruiser in front of the house and killed the engine.

Somewhere a dog howled.

They got out of the Ute, grabbed their bags from under the tray's tarp and headed for the house.

Talinga waited, dark and inexorable, splinters of light escaping its window edges.

'Strange,' Rob said. 'The place looked brighter when we were further away.'

'Maybe somebody closed the curtains.'

'Maybe.'

When they reached the door, Rob used the knocker. They looked at one another, waiting. From inside came the sound of approaching footsteps. The door opened and a man appeared holding a kerosene lamp high in one hand; behind him shadows danced. He was tall and thin, with shoulder-length hair. His handsome face was marked by lines of time and a jagged scar ran along his cheek bone. 'I take it one of you is the writer?'

'I am,' said Rob.

The men introduced one other.

Rob held Kieran's gaze. The caretaker's animalistic eyes were alert and dangerous-looking. 'I hope you're better at writing than keeping time.' Kieran moved aside, allowing the men to cross the threshold.

'We got caught in rain,' Cal said.

The caretaker stared, his mouth pressed into a thin line, then turned away.

They walked down the hall. Brass lamps illuminated several black and white photographs upon the walls, a few finely carved chairs, a sideboard table, and a large mirror in which their forms loomed large. At the hall's end, two doors stood opposite one another. Kieran turned left, leading them into another hallway that seemed even longer than the first. This passageway was lined with nothing more than closed doors.

Halfway down the hall, Kieran stopped and gestured towards two doors a few metres apart. 'Take your pick. The rooms are adjoined inside.'

'We won't need separate rooms,' Rob said.

'Please yourself. The bathroom's down the end of the hall. See you in the morning.' Shoulder stooped, Kieran walked back down the hall and disappeared.

'Strange guy,' Cal said.

'You think?'

'Definitely. Don't you?'

'He seems interesting.' Rob opened the door, explored the internal wall with his fingers and flicked a light switch.

The spacious room featured heavily draped windows and a double bed. A wing chair covered in dark velvet stood in one corner, and a dressing table topped with an oval mirror rested against the nearest wall.

Their bags landed on the floor with a thump.

Placing his keys on the dressing table, Cal said, 'This place must be worth a fortune.'

Rob pulled back the blankets and fell into bed. He watched as Cal tossed his shirt on the floor before switching off the light.

'What do you reckon?' Cal lay down beside him.

'About what?'

'Being here — everything?'

'It's something we'll never forget.' Rob closed his eyes and Kieran's piercing gaze flashed through his mind.

'Here's hoping you get a great story,' Cal said.

'Yeah.'

Rob lay still, listening to the steady rhythm of Cal's breathing, until sleep finally came.

The Garden

Alex sat on a wooden bench-seat, taking in the quiet. The garden was overgrown: eucalypts reached towards a blue sky, shrubs jostled for space amongst the long grass, and a knotted vine clambered across the hospital's peripheral stone wall.

This place came to him in a recurring dream. Alex would be tied to a chair, hands behind his back, leaves tumbling by in a carpet of red and gold. He could hear constant whispering, but no clear words. Shafts of sunlight snuck through the trees, stroking his face. He was waiting for someone, but no one ever appeared. When he woke, loneliness would wash through him, drenching his insides. The dream made no sense. In the conscious world, the garden brought him peace and he went there regularly to draw. Then there was the vision of Our Lady he'd experienced in the garden three years earlier. She'd floated high in the branches, her colors bright and warm. He hadn't seen her since, but had drawn her over and over. She haunted him.

It was late afternoon and a soft light crept through the trees. The wind picked up, sending leaves drifting through the air. A gardener often wandered about; he was a short, overweight man, who walked with a rocking gait, his gaze pitched towards the ground. He mostly raked leaves, shoveled them into a wheelbarrow, then carted them behind the hospital. There was no sign of the gardener now; the place was deserted.

Alex leant back against the seat and watched as treetops swayed, their branches tracking sweeping motions. He sought out the gaps of blue. What unknown worlds were floating through space? Potentially billions. An awareness of his own insignificance helped relieve his anxiety. If he wasn't important, then nor were his troubles — they were nothing.

He ran a finger along the bench seat, tracing the scalloped edges of peeling paint. His body had responded well to treatment and the chances of achieving remission again were solid, but he remained scared as hell. His social worker, Miss Jennings, said fear was designed to strengthen his fighting spirit, but the idea didn't lend much comfort. He couldn't help wondering if the cancer was still lurking deep within his cells. Alex knew that for every ten ALL sufferers, two lost the battle early on. With the relapse, his chances of survival had dropped to around sixty percent. If the disease were to reappear in his bone marrow, the odds of survival would be minimal.

Closing his eyes, he tried to forget that for nearly two months his survival had been linked to automated routines. It was time to unplug from machines. Alex tuned into the surrounding sounds. The wind sighed, birds nattered, traffic murmured. He looked to the tree where Our Lady had once appeared, but saw only dappled light.

Movement flickered at the edge of his vision. On the ground a stout bearded dragon basked in the sun. Its grey and rust-coloured skin blended with the leaves, but its spikes shone like metal spurs, spoiling the camouflage. Standing with its tail jutting skyward, the lizard danced. The creature lifted a front leg and traced a circle in the air, before resting it on the ground and lifting the other. On and on it danced, its jagged armor glinting with splintered light.

Alex watched, mesmerized. The lizard's movements seemed mechanical, yet ritualistic. A bulbous eye sparkled as the creature tilted its head. It froze, one leg thrust above its head, claws splayed. Time seemed to stop; Alex longed to be like the lizard, immersed in the present moment. He heard bracken breaking, leaves crunching, and the lizard darted from sight. Alex turned and saw Kelly Faulkner approaching. His heart worked hard inside his chest. She could never be his. It was time to let go.

Kelly walked amongst the trees, her figure projected onto a screen of leaves. She wore a sheer dress and Alex saw the swell of her hips before turning away.

She reached him, sat down and took hold of his hand. Alex glanced at her knees, which were pale and smooth.

'Long time no see.'

She smiled. 'It's only been two days. Miss me?'

'Yeah.'

'We can make up for it when you come home.'

'I need to take it easy. Doctor's orders.'

She touched his cheek. 'How you feeling?'

'Okay.'

'Is the medicine still making you sick?'

'Not anymore.'

'You excited about getting out?'

'Of course.'

'Not long now.' She rested her head on his shoulder. 'Then we can spend more time together.'

'There's something I have to tell you, Kell.'

'What?'

'I want to go away.'

She straightened up. 'Where?'

'The Doc's mother lives down at Pegasus Bay.'

'But that's four hours' drive south.'

'More like three.'

'When will you be leaving?'

'Next week.'

She crossed her arms. 'Can't wait to go, huh?'

'It's not like that.'

'Then how is it, exactly?'

'The Doc's mother draws. She's supposed to be pretty good.'

'And?'

'I was hoping she could teach me something.'

'What about going to uni?'

'I've already told you, it's not for me.'

'There's an art college up north as well,' she said.

He stared at the stone wall ahead.

'Why is it you're determined to move in the opposite direction to me?'

'Circumstances, I guess.'

Kelly sighed. 'Have you told your parents about heading south?'

'Not yet. I'll tell Mum soon.'

'What do you think she'll say?'

'I don't know.'

She gripped his hand. 'I've heard it's nice down that way.'

'Me too.'

'How long will you be gone?'

'A few weeks. Maybe a month.'

'Aren't you rushing things a bit?'

'What makes you say that?'

'I thought you'd stay put a while.'

'Why?'

She shrugged. 'I don't want anything to go wrong.'

'Jesus, Kell. Anything can go wrong, anytime.'

'Are you scared?'

'Yeah, but I can't let that stop me from taking a chance.'

'I'm going away, too.' Kelly traced the blue lines on the back of his hand.

'I know.'

'Doesn't it bother you?'

He ran a hand over his scalp, feeling the prickles of new growth. 'You've worked hard to get into uni.'

'But we'll be apart.'

'Not forever.'

Silence sidled up between them.

She stood. 'I should go. I'll come see you at home.'

'Okay.'

Alex watched her walk away; the contours of her body were visible through her dress and made his insides ache.

He looked over to the lizard's sunning spot, but the creature remained hidden as shadows swung across the ground.

The Bell Tower

The bell tower stood fifteen meters high and had been built as a separate structure behind the homestead. The three men stood near the tower's makeshift window, which was no more than a square hole in the brick work. The view stretched west across a sea of desert, with hardly a tree visible beyond Talinga's borders.

Rob shielded his eyes against dust kicked up by a hot wind and looked out over the window's ledge. Far below, a tin shed glinted in the sun; there was a pile of timber in front of it, along with odd bits of rusted machinery. Pulling back, he steadied himself against the wall.

Cal stood facing the huge bell. He walked forward, grabbed the rope and pulled hard. The bell swung from side to side, its sound deep and sorrowful.

'So what did old John want something like this for?' Rob asked. 'It's not like there's anyone nearby to hear it.'

Kieran shook his head. 'No one knows.'

'Maybe it gave him a reason to come up and enjoy the view.' Cal stared out across the desert.

'I heard a priest died up here,' Rob said.

'Yeah. Patrick Flanagan.'

'He jumped, right?'

'Bingo.'

'Why do you think he did it?'

'Some say he was tormented by Vanessa's ghost, who wanted him to spill the beans about her husband's murderous ways. Others believe he'd simply had enough of life — it happens.'

'So which version of events is true?'

'What difference does it make?'

'I want to get the facts straight,' Rob said.

Kieran laughed. 'Good luck. The stories about this place are always changing, like they've got a life of their own.'

'Somebody must know what happened.'

'Maybe, but they're most likely six feet under by now.' Kieran crossed his arms and leant against the wall. 'I know one thing for sure.'

Looking at the bell through his camera, Rob took a shot. 'What?'

'Patrick Flanagan died exactly one year to the day after Vanessa and Albert disappeared.'

Cal glanced at Kieran, but kept quiet.

'Christ,' Rob said. 'That's bizarre.'

'Is it too bizarre to be a coincidence? That's the question.'

'Do the present owners think the place is haunted?'

Kieran shrugged. 'I wouldn't know. They're hardly ever here, always travelling.'

'They must be wealthy.'

'Very.'

'And what about you?' Rob said. 'Ever seen anything strange? Any ghosts?'

'That would be telling.' Kieran spoke over his shoulder as he walked towards the stairs. 'Tomorrow we'll head to Patterson Creek, where Vanessa and Albert died.' Then he was gone.

Rob and Cal stood in silence as the wind howled.

Our Lady: A Vision

The figure of Our Lady shimmered in the afternoon light. Standing beneath the tree in which she'd appeared, Alex stared in silent ecstasy. She seemed to emit pulsating waves of warmth, and he understood things were as they were meant to be. Our Lady was watching over him. He tried to speak, but words eluded him. Tears blurred his sight. Alex blinked, and still she remained visible, gloriously ablaze. Our Lady smiled, and it was as if all the anxiety he'd ever experienced miraculously vanished.

Trees whispered to one another, sharing secrets. Stepping forward, he waited.

'It will be all right,' she told him. 'Everything will be okay.'

'How do you know?'

She smiled, but didn't answer.

Alex raised a hand, but she was too high to reach. He trembled as his veins swelled with reverence. His legs grew weak and he fell to the ground. The sky above was an endless blue field waiting to be explored.

Letting go, he felt himself sink into the warm earth and down through its center, so that his body

burned with fever. Cool air rushed against his face as he slipped through the planet's underbelly.

Then he was floating in space.

You're not alone, a voice said.

Is that you? he asked. *The Mother of Mercy?*

Yes. Don't be afraid. Her voice was hardly more than a whisper. *I'm here.*

The sun burned fiercely, outshining all other stars. The earth drifted further away and its oceans merged into a beautiful swirling blue. A lone satellite sailed past, panels gleaming with electromagnetic radiation.

Where am I going? he asked.

Home, she said. *Not long now.*

With his limbs spread and his eyes closed, he drifted on, finally at peace.

Patterson Creek

Rob lay sprawled on a rock, the sun's warmth making him drowsy. He could hear someone swimming below.

Water babbled as it slid past.

Haunted or not, Patterson Creek was a place of breathtaking beauty.

Moments later, he smelt cigarette smoke and knew Cal was out of the water. They hadn't spoken much since arriving at Talinga; their words came out wrong and bruised.

What was this thing that existed between them? What had it become? As far as he could tell, there were no answers.

The quiet embraced him, lulling him to sleep, where he teetered on an invisible edge before plummeting through space. Terror flooded his veins as he woke with a jolt. Rob sat up, his hands resting against warm rock, chest heaving.

Kieran was seated beside him, shirtless, skin glistening in the sunshine. His hair was wet and stretched past his shoulders, curling up at the ends. 'Bad dream?'

'Yeah.'

'I can empathize — I have nightmares a lot.'

'What about?'

Kieran shrugged. 'All sorts of things, but mostly hell. That place plagues me.'

'What's it like? In your dreams, I mean.'

'Cold and empty.' Kieran turned and Rob saw that the scar on his face had turned a fresh pink. 'Nothing but white cliffs and ice, everywhere ice.'

'Isolation's not good for a person. Maybe you've been alone too long.'

'Maybe I have.'

Rob leant forward, scanning the water below. 'Where's Cal?'

Kieran gestured towards the other side of the creek. 'Gone exploring.'

'Let's hope he doesn't get lost. When did he leave?'

'A few minutes ago.'

Rob turned at the sound of a crow. The bird sat in a nearby tree, its black feathers almost green in the afternoon sun. Glancing back at Kieran, he noticed his ribs were like little ridges beneath the skin. What would they feel like to touch?

Touch.

The word quivered, bright orange behind his eyes.

'What are you thinking about?' Kieran said.

'Nothing.'

'You must've been thinking about something.'

'Okay, I was thinking about a word.'

'Which word would that be?'

'Touch.'

'Touch?'

'Yeah. The weird thing is, I was seeing the word as I thought it.'

'What do you mean?'

'Words take on certain colors and shapes inside my head.'

Leaning back on his hands, Kieran crossed his ankles. 'Sounds like you've taken too many drugs.'

'If only it were that easy to explain. This sort of thing's been happening since I was a kid.'

'Seriously?' Kieran looked at him, his lips forming a crooked line.

'Yeah, it's called synesthesia?'

'I've never met anyone like you before. Cal's a lucky guy.'

Rob ignored him.

The creek murmured beneath them.

'I've got information that might interest you,' Kieran said.

'Like what?'

'Things about Talinga, about people who used to live there.'

'Who?'

'Vanessa Clark. I found her diary a while ago. It contains plenty of secrets.'

'What's the catch?'

'What makes you think there's a catch?'

'Nothing comes for free.'

Kieran brushed a bug off Rob's arm; it flew away, blue wings shimmering. 'I don't want much, just a bit of fun. Like you said, isolation's not good for a person.'

It was tempting. Christ, with the right information, he'd have editors eating out of his hand. 'I thought you were straight.'

'Things aren't always black and white.' Kieran lay back on the rock, put his hands behind his head and closed his eyes. 'Maybe you should think it over.'

Rob let his gaze climb over Kieran's body before getting to his feet. Across the creek, framed by a sky of dazzling blue, Cal stood watching.

The River

The quiet of Dr Knowles' office provided relief from the constant thrum of activity on the hospital's lower floors. Outside, giant slabs of glinting glass scraped the sky. The city's river ploughed eastward, sliding beyond a pile of concrete; the sight made Alex sick with longing in a way he didn't understand.

Seated beside one another, he and Edie McKenzie waited. The air was cool and musty. His mother regularly glanced towards the door. Alex envisaged her anger as a sea of red waves that slapped against the walls. He'd told her about his plans to head south as they walked to their appointment. She'd torn shreds off him, giving him every possible reason not to go, and now they shared an unnerving silence. Alex didn't look forward to hearing what she had to say to the Doc.

The whir of machinery located on the hospital's rooftop drifted through the ceiling. As he listened, Alex saw giant fan blades inside his mind; they spun slowly, carving up the light. The impression wired itself into his consciousness. Like monsters, images of machines — intricate and dark, with intertwined tubes and a multitude of sharp metal edges — featured strongly in his dreams and drawings.

He closed his eyes and waited for his head to clear.

The Doc had taken him up to the roof not so long ago. With an orange sun hanging low in the sky, they'd looked over the city, watching as a trail of cars lurched through the streets. Perched above the world like that, Alex could breathe right.

He looked around the room, absorbing its silence. Bookshelves jammed with medical texts lined the side wall. The Doc's desk was almost empty. His gaze moved from a neat pile of papers to a telephone, then the gleam of polished wood. The ticking of a large clock on the wall stabbed at the quiet.

The door flew open and Dr Knowles marched in. 'How is my favorite patient today?'

'Glad to be alive, I guess,' Alex said.

The Doc smiled. 'Spritely, I see. That's good.' He sat on his swivel chair, wheeled forward, then placed his forearms on the desk. 'And you Edie? I trust you're well?'

'Yes, thank you.' She clasped her hands together in her lap. 'Alex tells me you two have had some interesting discussions of late.

'Many. Your son is an interesting fellow.'

'Can you fill me in on his plans to go away?' Edie's voice trembled. 'I believe it was your suggestion?'

The Doc's gaze slid to Alex, then back to Edie. 'I mentioned it during one of our conversations, yes.'

'You just happened to mention it might be a good idea for him to head south, before speaking with me?'

'Perhaps I should have discussed it with you first.'

'It's a bit late for that.'

'What are your concerns, Edie?'

'I'm worried about Alex leaving town so soon after his relapse. It's asking for trouble.'

Dr Knowles leant back in his chair. 'I understand, but Alex is in consolidation and his immunity is stable.'

'What if he needs medical attention?

'Pegasus Bay has a hospital.'

'Apparently the plan is for him to stay with your mother?'

'That's right — Molly Knowles. I could arrange for her to contact you. Alternatively, I can give you her number.'

She drew in a breath. 'Why would Alex want to stay with someone he doesn't know when he can come home with me?'

'My mother's an artist. She could help Alex refine his drawing skills.'

Edie turned to Alex. 'We can arrange for you to take drawing lessons here. I'll look into it straight away.'

'No, Mum.'

The phone rang and Dr Knowles answered it. 'Yes? Tell him I'll call back. Thank you.' He hung up the receiver, lifted a hand and spread his fingers wide. 'We're all on the same side here. I'm sure we can work this out.'

'He needs stability right now,' Edie said.

'Mum, I'm not a child anymore. Besides, Miss Jennings said it would be a good idea for me to go someplace different.'

'You're only seventeen and you're sick. Now's not the time to be going away.'

'But I want to lead a normal life.'

His mother bit down on her lip, then said, 'Normal is applying for university, like Kelly and your other friends.'

Looking out the window, he caught sight of a lone eagle. It flew towards an adjacent building and landed on a ledge about twenty floors above street level.

'I really think Alex could do with a change,' the Doc said. 'I've continued close surveillance for the last few weeks, when he could have been treated as an out-patient. He'll be fine to take a short trip.'

'What do you call short?' Edie asked.

Dr Knowles shrugged. 'A few weeks.'

'There'll be no problem with him receiving hospital care in Pegasus Bay if necessary?'

'None that I can foresee.' The Doc placed his hands on the arms of his chair. 'He can take oral medication from here on. The tumor has been eradicated and, as you both know, there's no sign of leukaemic marrow involvement.'

Out amongst the concrete, cranes jerked and tilted, their metal limbs shining in the sun.

The clock ticked.

'You'll be discharged tomorrow, Alex. I expect you back in town within four weeks for a check-up.'

Clutching her handbag, Edie stood. 'Get well, Alex. Do you hear me?'

He nodded.

She walked towards the door and spoke without turning. 'I'll see you in the morning.'

Alex shifted in his seat. 'Okay.'

Edie's skirt whirled as she rounded the corner and disappeared into the corridor.

Afternoon: A Memory

Tearing along the highway, windows down, they headed for Patricia Taylor's place.

It was a hot Summer's afternoon.

'Let's take a detour,' Cal said. 'I want to show you something.'

Rob grinned. 'Can't wait.'

'Your mind's a sewer.'

Cal veered down a dirt road that ran parallel to a row of trees. The vegetation twisted and turned, marking the path of a waterway. They pulled over and got out of the Ute.

'This way.' Cal cut through a curtain of foliage.

The ground was cool beneath Rob's bare feet, the leaves soft. A slab of water slid past, its surface mottled with shadows and reflected light. Across the river, trees swayed.

Cal removed his glasses, kicked off his boots and undressed. 'I used to swim here as a kid.'

Rob peeled off his clothes. 'Shown this place to any other lovers?'

Cal grinned. 'Wouldn't you like to know.'

Rob stepped towards the river's edge, turned, stretched his arms above his head and back-flipped into the water. On the opposite bank, a cloud of cockatoos rose above the tree tops.

Cal held his breath as he watched the water.

Finally, Rob burst into view, hair slick against his skull.

'Haven't you heard of submerged hazards?'

'What?'

'You could have broken your neck.'

'Relax, would you?'

'It's hard when you do crazy shit like that.'

'Stop stressing and get in here.'

Cal took a few steps into the water, then plunged beneath its surface; he came up gasping. 'It never used to be this deep.'

'Things change.'

'Maybe, but you're still crazy.'

Rob duck-dived, opening his eyes against the turbid water. Swimming deep, he reached the bottom of the river, grabbed a handful of tiny stones, and headed back for air. A yellow circle floated above, its edges glowing. At the surface, he let out a roar that bounced off the trees.

'What the hell are you doing?'

'Checking the depth. It's got to be close to ten feet.' Rob opened his hand, letting the stones fall. 'Can't see a thing down there.' He climbed out and lay on the grass. Soon Cal was beside him.

Cicadas screeched.

'You know what I wish?' Cal said.

'What?'

'I wish I could be like one of those lizards. What are they? The ones that regrow their legs?'

'Salamanders.'

'Yeah, salamanders. Imagine that. Lose an arm, regrow it. Cop a hole in the heart, plug it. Never that simple, though, is it.'

'Nope.'

Cal sat up and glanced at Rob over his shoulder. 'I wish I knew how things were going to turn out.'

'What with?'

'With us.'

'What are you worried about?'

'Nothing. I just want to know we're going to be together.' Cal slipped into his clothes and put on his glasses.

'We are together.'

'For now. But what about tomorrow? What about next week?'

'What about it?'

'What happens then?'

Rob stood and stepped into his pants. 'You can't plan everything.'

'I know.' Cal lit a cigarette and blew a series of perfect smoke rings. 'But I was hoping we could share a flat or something. I'm earning a solid wage, enough to keep us afloat.'

Looking up, Rob saw a patch of blue through the branches. 'Life's pretty simple right now. How about we keep it that way?'

'Sure.' Cal began walking towards the car. 'Besides, who am I to complicate things?'

Disconnecting

Alex hovered in the doorway leading to the chill out room. The computer sat in the far corner, inert. He looked at its grey lines and sensed the strange pull of the electronic world. The clock on the wall showed it was after seven; the others would already be on-line.

He stepped into the room. No one else had come in yet, not even old man Boots. Sunlight poured through the window, spilling across the keyboard. There was no telling when he'd next be in cyberspace. It was time to pull the cord; he needed to get real and move on.

Alex pulled up a chair, logged in and scanned the exchange; his on-line buddies were talking about recent music festivals. He started typing.

I'm here to bare my soul and crash this cruisey conversation. It's my last week of therapy. Hope it's enough, but there's no guarantees. The good news is the cancer hasn't spread. The relapse was isolated to my gonads and the tumor has been wiped out. Apparently, it could have been worse. Ridiculous, but true. — Dog Star.

A response came through in seconds.

Nice 2 hear from u. Good news about the tumor. U still anxious about things? — Dark Angel.

Unsure of how much to tell, he kept his answer brief.

I've become better at managing the uncertainty, being more familiar with it. On the other hand, the stakes are high coz if I don't kick the cancer this time, than the prognosis will only get worse. Happy days! — Dog Star.

Alex was satisfied he'd disguised the feeling of emptiness that at times threatened to swallow him whole.

You're the bravest person I've ever come across. What I might do with a mere scrap of your courage. — Dark Angel.

What was he supposed to say? He didn't consider himself brave. So many things scared him, especially the unpredictable nature of his illness. It could recur and strike any part of his body, anytime.

There are people who care about me, who want 2 help. The thing is, I need 2 fight this battle on my own, so it's hard 2 let others in. I'm a king-sized prick most of the time. 1 day I'll probably go to hell. Which brings us back 2 a familiar topic. — Dog Star.

Dust motes drifted through the air, catching the light.

What's Myth Boy think about that raging inferno supposedly lurking in the bowels of some parallel world? Is there any room for redemption? — Dark Angel.

Dr Seuss entered stage left.

Depends on how u perceive hell. Is it a place of punishment solely 4 us sinners, or part of an entire world beyond ours? Early on, the Greeks spoke of an underworld where everyone went after life. They also believed in Tartarus, a place at the bottom of the underworld darker than anywhere imaginable. Ideas about people being thrown into Tartarus cropped up in Plato's stuff, *The Myth of Er*, and all that. Maybe that's where the idea of hell as punishment came from? Seems Christianity ripped off the ancient philosophers. – Dr Seuss.

Alex waited.

Are u saying this place of demons, boiling rivers, brimstone, and cleft-footed creatures stemmed from a story written well before Genesis? — Dark Angel.

I am. It seems many religious institutions have capitalized on the ancient fear associated with invoking the wrath of supposedly immortal beings. The idea of hell could be 1 of the biggest and longest running experiments in social control the world's ever known. — Dr Seuss.

He scrolled down the screen.

Nothing like a bit of conspiratorial thinking to spice things up. I don't believe in an underworld, but I'm convinced people, or souls, travel 2 different places after they die. Who knows where? It's a big universe out there. So while death can be scary, I think there's hope in it, 2. — Dark Angel.

Alex wanted to soak up her optimism, but fear nipped temptation in the bud. The idea of exploring otherworldly frontiers was almost overwhelming.

Dark Angel changed the topic before anyone replied.

How's that girl going, Dog Star? It's Kelly, right? — Dark Angel.

Alex was caught off-guard; reading her name left an ache inside his chest. He wanted to tell them that cutting the ties with Kelly seemed easier than hoping things would work out, but putting it into words was too hard.

It's a long story, but basically the fear of losing her is messing with my head. — Dog Star.

My sympathics. U must be close to scoring your home pass. When's the big move? — Dr Seuss.

2morrow...no more noises drifting in from long corridors at night. So I'll be detouring off the information highway 4 a while. Got some things 2 sort out. I'm sure we'll cross paths in cyberspace again, but 4 now it's adios amigos. — Dog Star.

Without waiting for a reply, Alex closed the window on his screen. He sank back in the chair and looked at the white ceiling, which seemed to shift like sand. Closing his eyes, he pictured Rob trekking across vast dunes, lost in the desert. The image vanished as quickly as it had appeared. It wasn't the first time Alex sensed trouble lying in wait for his brother. He'd been worried since hearing Rob had ventured west. Wary of his own imagination, which tended to be over-active, he'd kept his concerns to himself.

Alex stood and walked from the room. Above, fluorescent lights buzzed; he squinted against their brightness. A trolley stacked with plastic bottles and buckets had been left by the wall. The smell of disinfectant turned his stomach.

Boots appeared and came shuffling down the hall. Tall and lean, he walked against an invisible wind, shoulders hunched, a swath of grey hair swept back from his forehead. The old man lifted a hand as he tottered by, his blue eyes shimmering.

Alex waved back, a stone lodged inside his heart.

The Cellar

The stairwell leading to the cellar smelt like wet earth. Rob ran a hand along the stone wall as it curved through the darkness, turning in on itself, step after step. The walls seemed to draw near and he felt close to falling. Shutting his eyes, he bent over and placed both hands on his thighs. The camera around his neck swung back and forth. Footsteps drifted up the stairs, nudging his awareness. Rob straightened to see Kieran down in front, his body silhouetted in the torchlight.

There was just the two of them present. By the time they'd decided to head down to the cellar, Cal had gone off to explore the homestead's surroundings.

As they ventured further into the bowels of Talinga, Rob's lungs grew tight. Leaning against the wall, he felt its dampness through his shirt. Rings of darkness closed in, shrinking his vision, and soon he saw only pinpricks of light. He slumped to the floor, putting his head between his knees.

'You okay?'

'A little dizzy,' he answered.

'You want to turn back?'

Common sense broke through; he had to go on. A professional article required quality research. 'No, but I need to sit for a minute.'

When Rob's vision cleared, he saw Kieran waiting below. The pathway beyond continued its spiral descent.

'Not much further,' Kieran said.

Rob stood and steadied himself against the wall before continuing.

When they reached the bottom of the stairs, Kieran turned, his face aglow with torchlight. He then moved on and Rob followed him through the darkness.

The cellar was larger than he'd expected, the ceiling high; its long shadows reminded him of a cave. The air was hot and stale. The rough brick walls were lined with shelves that stored assorted jars, tools, pieces of scrap metal. There were things he couldn't quite make out, items the colour of ivory, patches of fur and leathery skin.

'What do you think?' Kieran said.

'It's like goddamn dungeon.'

Rob peered into the gloom, heading for the nearest set of shelves. He stepped back as torchlight pierced the darkness. Before him stood a row of jars, each containing some hideous specimen: a giant bug, a spider, a snake. There was also an array of stuffed animals. He recognized a crow, a possum a desert fox, several rats.

Walking the length of the wall, Rob stared at cramped legs, greasy feathers, shriveled pelts, and eyes that seemed to shine even in death. 'What is all this?'

'The remnants of John Clark's hobbyhorse. He was an amateur taxidermist.' Kieran flashed the torch upon the opposite shelves, where an equally large collection of specimens had been laid out. 'He thrived on collecting dead things, stuffing them and preserved, whatever a taxidermist does.'

Rob lifted his camera and started shooting; flashes lit up the gloom. 'I wonder what makes a person do something like that. It's so grim.'

'Why does anyone do anything? So many choices — some bad, a few good — it all equals a brown mush of human experience in the end.' Kieran picked up an old scythe and studied it as he spoke. 'They were filthy rich. I guess he thought preserving dead things was a valid way to use his time.'

'Christ, it's weird down here.'

'You think so?'

'Definitely.'

'Take a look at this.' Kieran stepped forward and shone the torch on a pair of chains attached to the back wall. Positioned roughly a meter apart and topped with rusty shackles, the chains slunk towards the floor.

Rob crouched low, taking more shots.

'This is where he kept her,' Kieran said. 'So the story goes.'

'What sort of sick bastard does that to his wife?'

'Who said anything about his wife?' Rob met Kieran's gaze and waited.

'There's more to the story than you think.'

'Such as?'

'This place was haunted before Vanessa and Albert met their fate down at Patterson Creek.'

'Who by?'

'The maid, Millie O'Sullivan. She was beaten by John Clark, then chained down here.'

'Why?'

'Maybe she wouldn't do the things he wanted. Who knows? The guy was a psychopath.'

Rob imagined desperate screams cutting through the quiet. Had anyone heard them? 'What happened to her?'

'Tried to escape in the middle of the night, took the carriage and raced off beneath a full moon. She lost control of the horses, ploughed into a tree and died alone in the middle of nowhere. No surprises. Her story was always going to end in tragedy.'

'She could have been happy, had things been different.'

'Nice thought, but not very likely given she was stuck in such an isolated place.' Kieran approached the closest set of shelves. He examined the skull of a small animal, then put it down. 'They say that whenever there's a full moon, a carriage appears outside the house just before midnight.'

'Have you ever seen it?'

'No, but maybe I choose not to. Around here it pays to keep a tight rein on your senses.'

Rob needed more information; he thought of the diary. Had Vanessa Clark recorded her husband's sadistic habits? Had she written about Millie? It must have been an electrifying read. 'So it's Millie's carriage people have seen?'

'Maybe. Maybe not. Here's where it gets really weird — Vanessa planned to escape on a night the carriage was due to appear. She thought it would be a good disguise, a way for her and Albert to leave without the noise of a carriage arousing her husband's suspicions. Not a bad idea, except escaping Talinga would prove to be more complicated.' Kieran's mouth curled into a smile. 'Legend has it that not long into the journey, Albert lost control of the carriage and plummeted into Patterson Creek.'

'So there was another fatal carriage accident?

'Yeah. I suppose it could have been a bizarre coincidence.'

'You don't sound convinced.'

'The second time round, no wreckage or bodies were ever found. Even the horses disappeared.'

'Strange.'

Kieran shrugged. 'I can't help thinking Millie had her revenge in the end.'

'By punishing Vanessa?'

'Apparently ghosts can be unforgiving.' Kieran gestured towards the chains.

'Vanessa knew what went on, but her hands were tied, so to speak. What could she have done? John Clark would have killed her had she blown the whistle. But somehow I don't think Millie's ghost would have been too sympathetic.'

'Maybe it's all speculation and rumor. Like you said, the stories are always changing.'

'I have evidence.' Kieran moved closer. 'The diary, remember? I found it amongst this junk.'

'What about Talinga's owners? Do they know you've got it?'

'No.'

'Don't you think you should give it to them?'

'What would they care? I'm the one who looks after this place. In a way, it's more mine than theirs.'

Rob stared; it struck him that Kieran was dangerously deluded. Is that what happened when a person lived alone too long? Did isolation skew perception to the extent that reality and fantasy became increasingly blurred? It was hard to know. There were too many grey areas. The man was an enigma residing in an equally mysterious place.

'I can show you the diary.' He clasped a hand around Rob's neck, pulling him forward. The camera lay between them, its edges hard and cold. 'Don't tell me you're not interested. Don't lie to me.'

Rob sucked air in through his nose.

Tightening his grip, Kieran moved closer and kissed Rob hard on the mouth. When he'd finished, he touched Rob's forehead with his own. 'Just a little piece of your soul. That's all I want.'

Rob closed his eyes. What would happen if he were to give in? What would it mean for his story? The information sounded invaluable. Nobody need know what he'd done to get it. Hearing something, he turned to look over his shoulder.

Near the bottom of the stairs, Cal stood holding a kerosene lamp, his gaze flitting between the men.

Explanations slipped in and out of Rob's mind, jamming his thoughts. 'It's not what you think,' he said, pulling away from Kieran.

Cal frowned. 'Then what is it?'

'Nothing. It's nothing.'

'Tell me,' Kieran glanced from Rob to Cal and back again, 'did you boys come all the way out here just to chase some stupid story. Is that really what you're after? Or is there something else going on? Something to do with pushing boundaries, going someplace neither of you have ever been?' Kieran pointed to his temple. 'Up here.'

Cal shook his head. 'I don't know what you're talking about.'

Stepping forward, Kieran lifted a hand and pushed Cal's glasses up the bridge of his nose. 'That's what you do, isn't it? You act innocent, like you don't know about certain things, but you know a lot more than you let on.'

'Get to the point. What do you want?'

'You know you're holding him back. You see, I have some information that interests your boyfriend tremendously. Here's what matters — how far are you prepared to go to let him have it? How much do you love him?'

'I don't need this.' Cal turned, then froze at the sound of Kieran's voice.

'Running away? Come on, be a real man for once. That's what Rob wants, someone with balls.' Kieran grabbed his crotch and grinned. 'I could show you how it's done. I was getting there, moving in. Who knows where we'd be now if you hadn't interrupted.'

Rob grasped Kieran's shoulder, spinning him round. 'That's enough.'

'Suit yourself. Maybe next time.' Kieran walked away and disappeared into the spiral staircase.

Silence filled the room as shadows clambered across the walls.

Rain

The metal eave outside Alex's bedroom hummed with the sound of rain. He walked to the window and looked through the gap between panes of frosted glass. Water spilled through the backyard. Thunder rumbled. Crossing to the bedside table, he reached around a cluster of medicine bottles and switched on the lamp. Alex glanced about the room. His computer sat on the desk, untouched since he'd come home. An open suitcase, mostly packed, lay on the bed. Tattered and scratched, the hard brown case was a relic of his mother's restless youth. He found it hard to imagine her as the roving gypsy she'd once been before meeting Brian McKenzie.

A cap of Rob's rested on top of the suitcase; it was green and looked like new. He'd had it since he was a kid, which was impressive. Rob was always losing things, or else forgetting where he'd left them; he wasn't much into material possessions. Two exceptions were his laptop and camera, both of which he'd bought in his first year at uni. It was only when operating these items that Rob seemed committed to being in the world. Otherwise, it was as if he floated above reality, refusing to let existence tie him down.

Alex saw his mother watching him from the doorway. There were shadows under her eyes, deep lines around her mouth. She'd been on edge, smoking and drinking too much.

'Have you heard from him?'

'Rob?'

'Who else?'

'No — he's probably busy.'

'No doubt.' She walked to the window. 'He'll have the bug now.'

'What do you mean?'

'The need to keep moving. You can box it up, shelve it somewhere, but it never goes away. It gets under your skin.'

The bed squeaked as Alex sat down. 'We always knew his career would keep him on the move. That's how it is for most journalists.'

'Being on the road's not as romantic as it seems.' Edie wiped her eyes. 'I called Patricia Taylor. She's heard from them. Cal said they're okay. That's something, I guess.'

'He'll be home soon.'

'I don't think your father's got a clue about what's going on between those boys.'

'Does it matter?'

'Nothing matters to him.' Leaning against the wall, she crossed her arms. 'I wonder what it's like to switch off the way he does and not worry about anything. Quite liberating, I'd imagine.'

'Dad doesn't seem too liberated.'

His mother glanced at the suitcase. 'Almost ready?'

'Almost.'

'I did the same at your age, travelled up and down the coast.'

'You shouldn't worry.'

'I can't help it. I'm your mother.'

Alex ran a hand over his prickly scalp; the hair was growing back fast. 'The Doc said my consolidation's solid, remember?'

'Yes.' Edie reached for Rob's cap. 'Where'd you find this?'

'In his cupboard. I felt like having something of his with me.' Alex shrugged.

'Figured he wouldn't mind.'

'Do you miss him?'

'Sometimes. At least he's out there chasing his dreams. People talk about that sort of thing, about what they'd do if they had the chance. Rob just does it.'

'I know. He's got no fear, which is bloody dangerous.'

'He'll be okay.'

'I hope so.'

Thunder rolled around the house.

'I remember when I bought this,' she said, looking at the cap in her hands. 'We were on holidays at Eight Mile Beach. You were both young, around eight and ten years old. It was the last family holiday we ever had. Do you remember?'

'Yeah, we nagged you for stuff. You got Rob the cap and me some goggles.'

'That's right, but you hardly used them.' His mother stared into space. 'For some reason you didn't want to swim anymore.'

Alex kept quiet.

She placed the cap on his clothes. 'You've told Kelly about the trip?'

He nodded.

'Was she okay?'

'She's disappointed. I think she expected me to head north to study.'

'Is that such a bad idea?'

'Let's just say it wouldn't work right now.'

'You might feel differently when you come back.'

'Maybe.'

The rain grew heavier. Edie walked to the window, grabbed the hook at the bottom of the frame and slammed it shut. Levering the other pane more gently, she stared at the frosted glass.

Alex stepped forward and placed a hand on her shoulder. 'I'm not going forever.' Edie nodded. 'Promise me you'll be careful.'

'Sure.'

She forced a smile, then walked from the room.

He lay down and stared at the ceiling, noting where the paint was peeling off in curled strips.

Regret

Rob stood in the doorway, uncertain of what to say. What had he done?

Cal zipped up his bag, lifted it off the bed, and moved towards the door.

'Why are you doing this?' Rob asked.

'I don't want to be here anymore.'

'Why not?'

'I don't like what's going on.'

'Nothing's going on.'

'You were kissing him.'

'No, he kissed me.'

Cal adjusted his glasses. 'That's not how it looked.'

'What do you mean?'

'Seemed like you were enjoying it.'

Rob said nothing.

'Be honest, how far would you go to get what you want? Would you kick me out of the picture if it meant nabbing a fantastic story?'

'It's not that simple.'

'Yes, it is. It is that simple. You either love somebody or you don't.' He let out a breath. 'And I don't think you've ever really loved me.'

'That's not true.' Rob reached out to touch Cal's chest. 'Please, don't go.'

'I've made up my mind.' Cal held his gaze, then stepped into the hall.

Rob sat on the bed and watched the curtains twirl in the breeze. Turning to look at the wing chair in the corner, he spotted his lap-top and camera.

If this was how things were going to be, then he needed to make it worthwhile.

Machines: A Dream

They sat by the sea, which glittered with sunlight. Alex felt Kelly's hand on his shoulder and turned. Her lips moved, but he couldn't hear a word.

Turning to the sky, he looked into a window of endless blue. High above, two eagles spiraled towards the water, talons interlocked. Further and further they fell. He pointed them out, but Kelly wouldn't look; she covered her face with her hands.

An eagle's cry pierced the air.

Why wouldn't she look?

Moments before impact, the eagles untangled themselves and looped upwards, heading for the sun.

Without warning, a hole appeared in the ground and he was tumbling through space. Peering over the edge, Kelly screamed and stretched out a hand.

Her eyes, the colour of sky and sea, they killed him.

A shadow crept across her features and the round light of her face contracted to the size of a pinhead.

Then she was gone.

A hot wind buffeted him as he looked down. Far below, deep in the earth, metallic forms gleamed. A low, mechanical hum boiled in the air. Except for the machines, he was alone.

They were waiting for him, cold and silent in the dark. Fear gripped his throat.

Landing softly in waist-deep water, he realized he had wings and that for some time he'd been drifting, not falling. A dim light from an unknown source revealed he was trapped by towering rock walls.

Had he died and gone to hell? He surveyed his surroundings. Enormous wheels churned through the water, intricately linked metal pipes disappeared into the walls, satellite dishes blinked, propellers apparently detached from crafts floated by.

The whir and thump of machines filled the quiet.

His pulse pounded.

A sorrowful voice rose above the sound of machines; someone was singing. He spun around, searching, but the sound seemed to come from every direction and he was unable to locate its source.

Alex cast an eye over himself; he was naked, his skin a shiny bronze. A metal button the size of a small coin sat above his heart. He pressed it and the button sank a centimeter or so inside his skin.

Golden beams shone from his eyes, lighting up the water. Rubbish floated by, plastic, cans, glass bottles, dead fish. There was even a human head. It drifted past, severed and bodiless, singing as it went. He grabbed a fistful of hair, lifted the head and saw it was Rob's. His brother's eyes stared dead straight. Alex screamed and let go; the head landed with a splash, but kept on singing.

He scrambled up the surrounding walls, wings fluttering as he leapt across ledges. A circle of light hovered above like a spaceship.

Reaching the surface, he climbed from the hole and looked around. There was no sign of Kelly. The beach was deserted and the sea was ablaze with a terrible, blinding light.

Haunted

The storm had worsened and a gale battered the homestead. Closed against the darkness, window panes rattled within their frames. Sitting in the study, fingers resting on his laptop, Rob tried to concentrate. He needed to get the story written. After days, he'd compiled no more than a few photographs and some rough notes. Apart from the snippets of information he'd received from Kieran, there wasn't much to go on. Rob couldn't have put his hands on Vanessa's diary if he tried. The caretaker had made himself scarce since the incident in the cellar.

While Talinga's history was grisly enough, he'd hoped to nail something more sensational, an exclusive eyewitness account of paranormal activity, but nothing had eventuated. He'd considered fabricating an incident or two — rocks inexplicably pounding on the roof, a luminescent figure appearing on the stairs — but it was an incredible risk. If he were exposed as a fraud, his writing career would be over before it even started.

In the corner of the room, the grandfather clock chimed; he'd spent hours getting nowhere.

Rob put his hand behind his head and spun around in the swivel chair. He looked at the walls, corners, ceiling. There was no sign of any ghosts. He noticed an unlit fireplace against one of the walls, and near this a gun cabinet. He returned his attention to the screen, willing the words to come, but drew a blank. The situation with Cal had shattered his focus. Sitting alone in a supposedly haunted house didn't help. It was only mid- afternoon, but the damp mist surrounding the homestead made it seem much later.

A sheet of white filled the room. In that instant, as lightning flashed, he glimpsed the outline of a figure through the window opening to the veranda. Thunder growled. Anxiety stabbed at his insides. Maybe Cal had come back? Rob crossed the room, unlatched the window and peered through the gap. The wind rushed in, along with the scent of rain.

Inspecting the veranda, he saw no one.

In the distance, a jagged line, white and fierce, ripped through the sky. A curtain of grey slid towards the homestead; it sounded like hooves pounding the earth. The curtain drew closer, the sound grew louder, then rain slammed against the tin roof. Rob looked up at the ceiling and imagined the homestead being swallowed by a sea of water. He was swimming in noise.

Returning to the desk, he stared at the laptop's screen. The cursor blinked.

Cal would be well on his way home by now. Christ, he missed him. He needed to get back and sort things out. He'd have Kieran take him to the nearest train or bus station in the morning.

But at what cost?

Rob pushed the question aside; there was still time to write. He started typing, punching out a few lines.

The clock chimed.

The keyboard clicked. Lines turned to paragraphs.

Without warning, a random stream of letters tumbled down the screen, slicing through his concentration. It must have been a power surge. He pressed the delete button, back-tracked up the page, then pulled the laptop's cord, letting it run on battery. White light filled his vision; a clap of thunder shook the quiet.

The screen flickered, turning bright, then dull. Rob watched and waited. How could an electrical storm affect a lap-top operating on battery? A swarm of static appeared on the screen. He slapped the desk; he hadn't backed up for ten minutes. Rob stood and walked away, hands on hips, his tread heavy upon the wooden floor.

Moving towards the study's side wall, he stared at a collection of framed photographs that had turned yellow with age. A somber cast of people long since dead stared back. The center of the wall featured a photograph of John and Vanessa Clark in front of the homestead, their expressions stern. Why had they married in the first place? Convenience? Combined wealth? No one would ever know.

The Clarks appeared in most of the pictures, along with several unknown faces — relatives or workers, maybe? There was no sign of children. He looked again at the central image of John and Vanessa. There was something about the picture he didn't like. An intense energy seemed to bear down on their faces and twist their features. Rob's vision blurred as the picture began to spin, slowly at first, then with more speed. His balance wavered and he shut his eyes, placing a hand against the wall. He focused on his breathing, determined not to lose consciousness, and the spinning sensation eased.

Looking again at the central photograph, he watched as a brown stain spilled out from Vanessa Clark's head. Fear ruptured inside his chest. He blinked and the mark vanished. Had he imagined it? Rob crossed the room, his heart thumping.

Rain hammered the roof.

He stopped a meter or so from the desk and caught a glimpse of something strange: two angular lines, joined at the bottom, cut through the screen, forming the shape of a 'V'.

He stepped forward, shoulders hunched, but saw only a host of shimmering pixels. Lightning flared in his peripheral vision as he eased himself into the chair. Rob was certain he'd seen something. Had it been a sign? A warning of some sort?

The rain eased and the wind died.

He walked to the window, legs shaking, and watched rays of sunlight pushing through clouds.

Out in front, Kieran's Cruiser glistened with raindrops.

He needed to clear his head, get outside and take some photos. A few pictures of the desert might capture Talinga's sense of isolation and spark his creativity. It had to be worth a shot. What was he waiting for?

South

The bus came to a shuddering stop and the driver announced their arrival at Pegasus Bay. The man beside Alex stood, retrieved a briefcase from the overhead locker, then moved into the aisle. Using his sleeve to rub mist from the window, Alex cupped a hand over the glass and peered out. It was dark and raining and the pavement shone with reflected light. He grabbed his backpack and moved up the front. His left foot tingled, messing with his balance. Outside, he stopped beneath the street light. An empty phone box stood nearby, its transparent walls glistening in the wet.

Wind swept through the night, blowing needles of rain into his face. The driver hauled luggage from the bus. Alex's suitcase landed on the pavement and he wandered over to it, then carried it back to where he'd been waiting. The bus had pulled onto a quiet service road behind the main drag. Across the street, backing onto the highway, a petrol station gleamed like a strange spacecraft.

Was it raining where Kelly was?

People walked by. The air swirled with voices; laughter erupted, then fell flat in the damp. A car sped past and he watched as its tail lights faded to little specks.

Loneliness swamped him. Why had he left home? Then clarity returned: to escape, to forget Kelly, to find a place where he could breathe.

Someone was moving towards him, their head hidden beneath a hood of a wet-weather jacket. As the figure drew near, Alex recognized the jutting cheekbones and sharp chin from the photos of Molly Knowles Doc had shown him.

She pushed back her hood, revealing long silver hair. 'Alex McKenzie?'

'That's right.'

'I'm Molly.' Lines huddled around her eyes as she smiled. The pair shook hands. Molly was lean and tall, like her son.

'It's good to finally meet you,' Alex said.

'Likewise.' She pointed to the case. 'That all you've got?'

'Yeah, that and my backpack.'

'I like a person who travels light.' Molly started crossing the street. 'Come on. My truck's this way.'

Gravel crunched beneath their shoes. The rain had stopped and Alex breathed in the warm night air. Tomorrow he hoped to go exploring, then draw for hours. He'd make his own choices, like his brother. Thinking of Rob made Alex's stomach tighten. He couldn't shake the feeling his brother was headed for a fall.

Alex looked back at the phone box. He wanted to hear Rob's voice, but who would he call? He didn't know where his brother was staying.

'You all right?' Molly was watching from the shadows ahead.

'Yeah, just a little tired.'

He ditched his bags into Molly's dual-cab, then climbed in the front. The vinyl upholstery was cold and smooth. Molly started the vehicle, hit the accelerator and pulled onto the road. The highway was poorly lit and Alex stared into the night. Further south, the coastline was speckled with lights, signaling the presence of suburbia.

After several kilometers, Molly turned onto a rough, winding track. Alex gripped the side of his seat as they weaved through the darkness.

Before long, the headlights shone upon a compact timber house.

She switched off the engine. 'It's a little out of the way, but that's how I like it. I can get whatever I need in town. There's a doctor nearby, too, ten minutes down the road. A hospital not much further than that.'

Alex nodded. 'The Doc told me.'

'Henry?'

'Yeah.'

'It's funny hearing you call him that. Sometimes I forget he's grown up.' Molly eased herself out, walked around the truck and helped Alex with his bags.

They walked along a path lined by dripping shrubs, up a set of stairs and along a narrow porch.

The ocean boomed somewhere nearby.

Keys jangled as Molly wrestled with the front door; it swung open and Alex followed her across the threshold, ducking beneath a low-set architrave.

She flicked on a light.

Inside, it was warm and dry, and the timber floors were covered with rugs. He followed Molly down a hallway, glancing at sketches hanging on the walls.

'Bathroom.' Molly gestured to the left. 'Laundry and storage,' she added, tilting her head to the right. They reached a metal staircase that climbed into the darkness and she pointed upwards. 'Your room, my room, my study. You need to get changed?'

'No, I'm fine, thanks.'

She placed his backpack at the bottom of the stairs. 'Then drop your suitcase and come have supper.'

Alex did as he was told.

'By the way,' she said, 'the study is off-limits. I don't like anyone rifling through my stuff.'

'Okay.'

The hall opened into a kitchen and beyond that a small set of stairs led to a sunken living area. A wooden table flanked by bench seats was positioned near the left wall. The lounge room hosted a pot belly fireplace, an old lounge and a coffee table. A tall reading lamp glowed in the corner and a bookcase stood near the back door, its shelves crammed with pages. A clock made from a ship's helm hung on the wall. There were plenty of drawings around, mostly seascapes.

Alex approached the fireplace and saw coals glowing behind the glass.

Molly rummaged through cupboards and placed things on the kitchen bench. 'You can stoke that fire. There's paper and bracken in the basket near the bookcase.'

'Sure.' Opening the fireplace, Alex placed a piece of timber on top of the coals, then another. He closed the door and adjusted the flue, watching as flames leapt.

'I'll be with you in a jiffy,' Molly called. 'Baked beans all right?'

'Great, thanks.' Looking up, he saw that the fibro ceiling finished at the kitchen. From there the cabin opened up, revealing raw timber beams and the faint gleam of a tin roof. Spider webs hung from the rafters and ropes strung with shells dangled from different places.

'I don't know if Henry told you, but cooking's not my strong point.'

Alex examined a sketch of the sea during a storm. 'Well, you draw beautifully.'

Molly poured beans into a saucepan and lit the stove. 'Thanks. Some people talk about my art like it's a spot of fun, something to keep me entertained. They'll say stuff like, "How's that hobby of yours going?" Or, "It's good to keep your brain busy, therapeutic."' She leant against the bench, arms crossed. 'Therapeutic, my arse. More like hard work.'

'When did you start?'

'Drawing?'

'Yeah.'

'Pretty much as soon as I could hold a pencil. I was probably about three. How about you?'

'I was around eight or nine.' He sat on the couch and stared at the fire. 'At least, that's when I remember wanting to get better.'

'You're seventeen now?'

'Yeah.'

'That gives us something to work with. You ever had lessons?'

'No. They had extra art lessons at school, but they cost a fair bit.'

Molly glanced at him. 'Ahuh.'

'What about you? Did you go to art school?'

'Nope. I've been in Pegasus my whole life and there's no art school around here.' She ran the kitchen tap, filled a couple of glasses and carried them to the table.

Alex sank further into the chair and listened to the fire crackling.

Walking to the stove, Molly lifted the saucepan and poured the beans into a couple of bowls. 'You better come eat before you fall asleep.'

He crossed to the table.

'I don't eat real regular — it's my vice.' She put down their bowls and sat opposite him. 'I'll do dinner for you each night. At breakfast and lunch, you're on your own.'

'Sounds fine.'

They ate in silence, spoons clinking. Wind whistled through spaces in the roof's metal sheeting. Alex looked at the seaward wall, which featured a couple of push-out windows. In the center of the wall stood a timber door with a tarnished metal knob; the lock held a long, bronze key.

'One thing I want to tell you,' Molly said, 'is that the sea's a dangerous place.'

Alex nodded. 'I know.'

'Henry tell you about his father dying out there?'

'He mentioned it.'

'Michael took too many risks and it caught up with him in the end.'

'Don't worry, I won't be going in the water.'

'I'm not saying you can't go in, just be careful. Don't swim near the rocks, stay away from the cliffs, that sort of thing. Got it?'

'Yeah, no problem.'

'Good,' Molly stabbed at the air with a crooked finger, 'because the ocean can fool anyone.'

Breakdown

The Cruiser banged along the dirt, throwing up plumes of dust. Nabbing the vehicle had been easy; the keys were in the ignition. Rob only needed a few photos and planned to be back at the homestead before dark. He'd deal with Kieran then.

The vehicle slid to one side and fishtailed down the road. He gripped the wheel, spun it left, then right, bringing things under control. Rob remembered his father teaching him to drive on the outskirts of Sherbrooke. It hadn't been that long ago, five or six years, but it seemed like another life-time. He couldn't understand why Brian McKenzie had fallen apart. Was the problem something genetic? Could it have been prevented? Questions haunted him.

A bulging sun hovered in the sky.

Shrubs and grass fell away as the track widened. Sand dunes erupted in the distance. He was driving on an expansive plain that burned with brightness. Colors of the desert swamped his senses. If he ventured into the heart of the place, its energy might bleed into his writing and take it to another level.

Keeping his gaze fixed dead ahead, Rob saw the distant horizon was hemmed by purple mountains.

He could have kept driving forever — there was nothing to stop him. Glimpsing something in the sky, he leant forward. High above an eagle wheeled, its wings stretched wide, making him crave his brother's company. Since that day at Eight Mile, the sight of eagles always reminded him of Alex.

Spotting a lone tree off to the left, he pulled over, grabbed his camera and jumped from the vehicle; the terrain was soft. He trudged towards the tree, dropped to his knees and started shooting.

The tree was dead, its branches resembling gnarled limbs. How the hell had it ended up there?

Rob got to his feet, turned and froze. About fifty meters away, a small dog stood watching him with its head tilted down, eyes shining.

He raised his camera, took a shot, then stepped forward. Rob longed for the dog to approach, but instead it turned and ran. He watched it disappear over a dune.

Returning to the vehicle, he placed the camera on the passenger's seat and peered through the windscreen. There was no trace of the earlier storm. He started the car and planted his foot. The engine roared, but the Cruiser stayed put. Rob got back out and saw the wheels had sunk deep into the sand.

He slipped the gear stick into neutral and tried pushing, but it was hopeless — the car refused to move. Resting against the vehicle's hot metal paneling, he scanned the landscape. There wasn't another creature in sight. He was alone in the middle of nowhere, and soon nightfall would come.

Stymphalians: A Dream

Alex lay on the beach, staring into a deep blue sky. The lip of the ocean rushed up the sand, then slipped away again, its movement a rhythmic pulse. He was aware of the planet's constant motion and understood that time and space stretched an immeasurable distance. Longing to see the horizon, he tried sitting up but remained immobilized by the momentum of hurtling through the universe.

A breeze ruffled his hair and skimmed across his skin. Salt air seeped into his lungs. Alex relaxed and allowed his body to sink into the sand. He spotted half a dozen birds, flying high. With wings sprawled, the creatures circled above, their bronze beaks glinting in the sun. They had metal arrows scattered amongst their feathers and talons sharp as blades.

Lying against the wet sand, Alex shivered. He was aware of dread slipping through his veins.

He tried calling out, but released only a whimper; his throat was desert dry. His heart raced as the birds dropped in altitude. They'd tear him apart, leaving his bones to bake in the sun. As the birds circled above, hooks of terror plucked at his chest.

Sinking deeper into the sand, he listened to the hissing of the sea.

The back of his neck prickled. Reaching around, he discovered a cord attached to the base of his skull. He wriggled it free, leaving a moist hole filled with grit. The end of the cord was fitted with three metal prongs, each covered in blood and chunks of flesh. Splayed wires hung from its other end. The cord was roughly the length of his body. He ran his fingers along its grey plastic coating, examining it carefully.

What the hell was going on?

Fear pierced his heart.

There was a shrill cry and he looked skyward. Circling low, the birds were a vortex of arrows, spikes and blades.

No longer pinned to the earth, Alex stumbled to his feet. The creatures stared with black, gleaming eyes.

Lifting the cord above his head, he swung it like a lasso then let go. The cord wrapped itself around the neck of each bird, chaining them together. Sparks erupted and the creatures fell in an electrified heap.

He slumped to his knees.

With a thunderous boom, the sky cracked open, revealing an expanse of darkness that stretched forever. Fragments of blue rained down, sharp as glass.

Trying to escape was pointless. Having fought and lost, Alex would soon be impaled alongside the metallic birds. It was only a matter of time before his luck ran out.

Lost

Brightness pressed against Rob's eyes. Squinting into the glare, he sat up and rubbed his neck. The vastness of the desert struck him and his stomach contracted, becoming a tight knot at the center of his being. Stunted tufts of grass littered the landscape; other than that, nothing seemed to be alive.

Nearby, the dead tree stood like a silent sentinel.

Hot air rushed in through the window, whipping up sand. He grabbed his camera and took a shot of the landscape. Rob pushed open the driver's door, shifted his legs and stood. Stumbling towards the rear of the car, he searched for signs of a path, but found nothing. Wind had swept away the Cruiser's tracks, leaving him disoriented. He stared into the distance, at where the desert met the sky, his eyes watering. It could be weeks, maybe months, before anyone came this way. By then he'd be dead.

Sweat pricked his brow.

Stepping towards the vehicle, he lost his balance and tumbled over. The sky was a deep, impenetrable blue. Up there, countless satellites were in orbit, bouncing radio waves back to earth, but they were no good to him. He was isolated and beyond contact. This had become blatantly obvious the previous evening, when he'd lain across the back seat of the car and watched stars sliding across the sky. It hadn't taken much to imagine himself as a lone astronaut drifting through space, destined to burn up like a meteorite. The same sense of hopelessness returned to him now.

Rob closed his eyes and concentrated on the warmth seeping into his back. Sand squeaked against his ear as he turned to look at the Cruiser's partially buried wheel. Even if he were to somehow prise up the vehicle, it would soon become bogged again.

He got to his feet and eased himself into the car. Reaching for the water bottle, he took a swig, replaced the lid, then threw it back on the seat. Almost empty, the bottle glinted in the sun. He caught his reflection in the rear-view mirror and spoke aloud, 'You're screwed now.'

The wind grew stronger, stinging his eyes. He wound up the window, leaving a thin crack for air. The vehicle's metal sheathing banged in the heat.

Rob waited, then slept.

When he woke, the sun had slid half-way down the sky and the wind had died. He got out of the vehicle and started walking. High above, an eagle soared. He watched as it flew towards a distant mountain range, then disappeared from sight. Thoughts of his brother came to mind and loneliness bled through his chest. He'd done nothing to ease his brother's pain and failed to support him as he struggled with illness. The realization stopped him in his tracks. He bent over, gasping. It was too late to go back, too late to say sorry.

Staring out at the barren landscape, Rob headed for the horizon.

He staggered forward as the heat drilled into his skull. He had no clue how long it had been since he'd left the car. An imposing dune swallowed his vision. Rob began to climb, his boots sinking deep into the sand. He sucked in hot air, then released it through his teeth; it hurt to swallow. Stumbling on, he climbed higher. At the crest of the dune, he shielded his eyes against the terrible brightness, saluting the great expanse before him. Heat waves shimmered. The sun burned. Something at the base of the dune caught his eye and he ran down the sand, legs quivering. At the bottom, he found a bunch of white flowers, each one shaped like a little bell.

Rob dropped to his knees, picked a flower and placed it in his mouth. Sweet juice burst onto his tongue. His stomach churned as he ate the flowers, one by one. For some time thirst had overwhelmed all other sensations, now hunger returned. Wiping his mouth, he sat back and tried taking stock of things.

He was done for, any fool could see that.

The landscape was an endless burnt sea. He looked at the sky. What was out there? Astronauts? Aliens? There had to be something.

Rob dug himself a trench and lay down, the desert shining red behind his eyelids.

Freedom

The track to the beach was edged by creeping plants, their plump leaves slick with wax. Tall grass dipped and rolled in the breeze. The air smelt salty and the sea thrummed.

Branches waved as Alex passed through a stand of head-high shrubs. The vegetation thinned and the track opened into a gaping mouth of sand. He marched along the dunes, his backpack digging into his shoulders. Stopping to adjust his brother's cap, he looked out at the expanse of blue. Flecks of gold bounced off the water and he envisaged himself in a vast desert. His mind shifted to Rob. How was he coping out there? He supposed he'd find out soon enough.

Scanning the coastline, he understood why Molly was obsessed with drawing the place. Pegasus Bay was wildly beautiful.

The bay was long, its beach stretching towards rocky promontories in either direction. To the south, a rugged headland jutted into the ocean, its granite cliffs glinting. Positioned back from the precipitous edge, a lighthouse shone in the morning sun. The headland to the north slipped into the sea, terraced by rocks and ledges protruding at odd angles. The top of the northern headland was a wide grassy knoll that featured a small white building.

Streaks of cloud stretched across the horizon, tearing at the sky. The sight reminded Alex of the hallucinations he'd experienced in hospital; all those claws and blade-like body parts. He missed peeping into that strange world, where his imagination went wild. At least he had his folio — there the images were fixed.

He ran down the dunes, sand squeaking beneath his feet, and stopped near the water. The sea crept forward, bringing with it scallops of foam, then fell back once more.

Bubbles simmered near his feet.

Whispers floated on the wind, urging him in, but entering the sea was out of the question. The scars from that day at Eight Mile were indelible.

A bird's cry pierced the air. Shading his eyes, Alex spotted an eagle. It plummeted from the sky and dove into the water, re-emerging with a fish wriggling between its talons. Turning inland, the eagle flew directly overhead, showing off its white belly before disappearing behind the dunes.

Alex turned and followed the ocean's fringe, heading towards the lighthouse.

The Grim Reaper: A Dream

Rob wandered through the desert, alone. Night had come and specks of light punctured the darkness, slipping past in a silver blur as the universe turned. The beauty of the sky was a fist rammed down his throat. He sucked in air, then swallowed.

A telephone box stood in the middle of nowhere, around fifty meters away. Beyond this, in the distance, lights shone. Why had he been worried? All he had to do was phone the cops, let them know he was lost, and they'd come find him. Up ahead a cord trailed through the sand and he realized one end was hooked into the base of his skull. He tried removing it, but the metal prongs were buried deep inside his flesh.

Stars swung across the sky, threatening his balance.

Rob stared at the telephone box and noticed a dark figure behind the glass. Had it been there all along?

He walked forward, holding the cord as he went; it guided him to the telephone box, where it slithered beneath the glass. The figure inside wore

a dark hooded robe and Rob understood he had crossed paths with the Grim Reaper.

Holding the receiver to its ear, the figure turned, its face cast in shadow. Rob tried to speak but fear had taken hold, and only a groan escaped his throat.

The Grim Reaper raised a hand and touched the glass. Compelled by an inexplicable curiosity, Rob mirrored the action only to witness the entire structure vanish.

He turned in a circle, searching the landscape. There was no one around. Loneliness pressed against his soul. Who in their right mind would feel sad about the disappearance of Death?

As he looked to the sky and took in the stars, his brother's voice entered his head.

What does it all add up to? Alex asked.

Nothing, Rob said.

But how can that be? Because even nothing has to add up to something.

Damn it, Alex, you think too much.

Rob sensed his brother's presence slipping away. He reached into the darkness, knowing he was entirely alone.

The Girl

The girl sat on a rock by the ocean's edge, arms wrapped around her legs, her hair stretching half-way down her back. She'd appeared without warning as Alex followed the promontory that jutted into the ocean before curving its way south. He stood close to the cliff, watching from the shadows.

Behind him the lighthouse loomed. The water was calm.

Usually the beach was deserted and he was free to wander the dunes, or draw for hours. There was nothing to distract him. He'd completed more sketches since arriving at Molly's than he'd done in months.

Seeing the girl had been a shock. Against the backdrop of the ocean, she looked frail, vulnerable. He imagined approaching from behind, startling her, watching her tumble into the Pacific. If he retraced his steps, she might turn and see him slinking away. Neither scenario would make a good impression.

Should he stay or go?

Shifting the weight of his pack, he looked at the lighthouse, then back to the girl. Water rushed into a nearby gap, thumping its way through subterranean channels before erupting as a fine mist. Alex closed his eyes for a second, maybe two. When he opened them, the girl was staring over her shoulder. Her hair flicked about in the breeze, as if testing for danger. Even from a distance, he could tell she was beautiful.

Her gaze bore into his forehead. He raised a hand, held it in mid-air, then let it fall. The girl didn't respond. She looked about his age. Across the slippery rocks he clambered, crab-like, towards the sea. After what seemed like an unbearably long time, he reached her and sat down. Alex looked at her, then out across the ocean. A convoy of white lines rushed towards land; beyond this, the water stretched flat and wide.

'Who are you?'

The girl had a thin face and green eyes set wide apart. A web of barely visible blue lines crept beneath her cheeks.

'Alex McKenzie.'

'Do you often spy on people?'

'I wasn't spying.'

'Then what were you doing?'

He shrugged. 'I didn't know anyone was here. I saw you and stopped — that's when you turned around.'

'Likely story.' A smile crept across her face. 'I'm Rose McGovern.'

A wave slammed into the rocks, showering them with ocean spray.

She jumped up, her toes white against the dark rock. 'Come on — tide's coming in.'

Alex edged his way forward, following her towards the cliffs. Ahead, patches of pale skin caught his eye, but he was forced to concentrate on the rocks, wary of the barnacles protruding from their sides.

Rose moved effortlessly, as if barely touching the earth. Reaching the beach, she looked over her shoulder, then headed for the dunes. Alex jogged to catch up, the pack thumping against his back. Reaching the top of the dune, he sat beside her.

Somewhere a bird screeched.

'This place is amazing,' he said, gazing out to sea.

'I know.'

'Did you grow up in Pegasus?'

'Yeah.' She ran her hand across strands of grass bowing in the breeze. 'Where are you from?'

'Up north, Sherbrooke.'

'What brings you down this way?'

'I needed to get away for a while.'

'It's funny,' she said, 'people come here for holidays. I dream of leaving, moving somewhere new and exciting.'

'Don't you like it here?'

'It's okay, but I get restless.'

'I know what you mean.'

'Where are you staying?'

'With Molly Knowles.' He heard her take a breath. 'You know her?'

'Everybody knows everybody in Pegasus — it's a small town.'

'Right.' Alex watched waves breaking way offshore. 'You still at school?'

'No. I look after my dad now.'

Alex touched the brim of his brother's cap, lifting it slightly. Questions formed inside his mouth, but stayed put.

'What's in the bag?' she asked.

'Drawing gear.'

'What do you draw?'

'Anything. People, the ocean, monsters.'

'Monsters?'

'It's a long story.'

'Molly draws, too, right?'

'Yeah, she's teaching me.'

'That's cool.'

Silence slid in between them.

Rose stood and wrapped her arms around her waist. 'I've got to go.'

'I guess I'll see you down this way again.'

'I guess you will. Good luck with your drawing.'

'I could give you a lesson or two.'

'I bet you could.' She took a few steps back.

'Maybe we should meet again,' he hesitated, then added, 'some place.'

She smiled and pointed towards the northern promontory. 'How about up there?'

He turned to see the church on the hill. 'When?'

'Tomorrow.'

'What time?'

'Early. You can draw as the sun comes up.'

'Okay.'

Rose made her way along the edge of the dunes, before disappearing into the scrub.

Contact

Opening his eyes, Rob stared into the darkness. His head throbbed and his throat burned. It took some time for his vision to clear, and when it had, he watched as a star cluster merged into a single disc high above. The disc hovered in the night sky, flashing red and green. He sensed a rhythm in its pulsating lights, some elusive code that lay beyond his understanding.

The disc was a spaceship — that much was clear — but what did it want with him?

The craft darted to one side, then steadied itself before slowly descending.

Rob sat up in his trench, blinking, and crossed his legs. He was neither afraid, nor particularly surprised by what he was seeing. It struck him that this encounter had been meant to happen.

How had they known where to find him?

A hot wind stirred and Rob shielded his face from the swirling sand.

The craft made no noise as it landed; its lights dimmed, but continued to blink. The spaceship's door slid up and disappeared behind silver paneling. A cloud of light poured from the craft, tinting the air yellow.

Rob rose to his feet.

A humanoid creature appeared in the craft's doorway. Moments later, it stood before him. It had a large head, sloping black eyes, a slit-like mouth, small orifices for its ears and nose. Its skin was grey and hairless, and it appeared to be sexless. The creature raised a three-fingered hand, held it in front of Rob's eyes, then lowered it again.

Rob's skin tingled. How many humans had experienced contact with extraterrestrials?

The creature spoke without moving its mouth. *You are a long way from home.*

So are you. The response spilled from Rob's head, drifting up into the ether.

Further than you will ever know.

Where are you from?

The creature blinked its eyes. *There's no point in trying to explain. You would never understand.*

What do you want?

To run a few tests. All very simple. Nothing dangerous. If you will step into our ship, we can be on our way.

You want to abduct me?

The creature stared. *We are not scheduled to examine any more humans at present. We have filled our quota. However, if you come with us voluntarily, our superiors will be satisfied protocol has not been broken.*

You have protocols for that sort of thing?

Of course. We're not barbarians. There are universal laws to heed.

Rob saw another creature watching from the ship's doorway. *I don't want to go.*

That may be so, but you appear to be lost. I could take you wherever you want.

Again Rob glanced towards the ship; the other alien raised a hand, displaying three fingers silhouetted against the light. He looked back to the creature before him; its gaze burrowed into his forehead and he shut his eyes. When he opened them, the alien had returned to the craft and was standing beside his companion.

Both creatures stared at him, but only one communicated. *Beware of turning back.*

What did you say?

Return at your peril.

What's that supposed to mean?

I don't know. I am simply relaying the message.

What message?

We must go. The alien turned away as the door slid down into place. The spaceship's lights grew bright. A hot wind blew once more and the craft rose above the desert. It stopped several hundred meters overhead, hovered without a sound, then sped off into the blackness of space.

Rob watched the disc until it disappeared amongst the stars. *Beware of turning back.* The words looped through his mind.

He swayed, then fell on his back, seemingly pinned to the earth like a scientific experiment.

Miss Jennings: A Memory

Alex usually met with his social worker in the garden, but it had been raining all morning so they agreed to talk in his room.

'Being heard is an essential part of being happy,' she told him. 'If that means talking on-line, that's fine.'

'Okay.'

Miss Jennings had black hair and smooth olive skin. Her eyes were the darkest he'd ever seen.

Alex adjusted his beanie. 'I'm not sure I know what happiness is anymore.'

'You once knew?'

'Maybe when I was little, around six or seven.'

'If there was one thing you could have today that you had when you were younger, what would it be?'

He listened to voices drifting in from the corridor, then said, 'It's probably what I didn't have that counts.'

'Such as?'

'Fear. I wasn't scared of anything.'

Miss Jennings wrote in her notebook. 'And now?'

'I suppose I'm easily spooked.'

'For what it's worth, I don't think so. In any case, a little fear can be good. It helps keep us safe.'

'Sometimes I feel like it's smothering me. Then I think, to hell with it. I'm going to be scared no matter what, so maybe I should take more risks, live a little.' Alex stared at the floor. 'That's what Rob does.'

'You think he's happy?'

'Probably not.'

'What makes you say that?' she asked.

'I don't know — a lot of the time he seems pissed off with the world.'

'What about you? Are you pissed off with things?'

'Sometimes. It depends on where my head's at.'

She leant forward, her elbows resting against her thighs. 'You need to stay positive, Alex. You know prayer can help, right?'

'I haven't been praying much lately, to tell the truth.'

'Why not?'

'Can't seem to find a good enough reason.'

'What reason do you need?'

'A sense it will make a difference.'

'But you have to *believe* in it — otherwise, what's the point?'

He shrugged.

'Let me ask you something,' she said, sitting back. 'How many nerve cells are in the human brain?'

'Around one hundred billion.'

'Right. The brain's billions of neurons connect with one another in incredibly complex networks, sending messages to all parts of our body so that we can function, physically and mentally. Do you really think this all comes down to chance, that it's some kind of random outcome?'

'I don't know. I'm a little confused right now.'

'Would you like to speak with someone about how you're feeling?'

'Who?'

'A priest comes to the hospital once a month. I could arrange for you to meet with him.'

'No, it's fine.'

She held his gaze. 'Okay, but remember to stay connected. Don't isolate yourself.'

'Sure.'

Miss Jennings made her way towards the doorway, then turned around. 'There's always hope, Alex'

'I'll try to remember that.'

Once she'd left, Alex looked through the window to where fragments of cloud peppered the blue. If he were a bird, he'd fly straight out and go wherever he wanted.

The Stranger: A Memory

Outside the spare room, Rob's feet were anchored to the floor. He gripped the door handle, straining to listen. Earlier, he'd heard strange noises — they'd lured him down the hallway — but now it was quiet. Maybe his mother had fallen and hurt herself?

He pushed against the door and peered through the gap.

Inside the room, candles burned and lace curtains lifted in the breeze.

Edie McKenzie lay on the bed, facing the window, her skin smooth and pale. Rob's chest tightened.

Beside his mother, a man lay with his head propped against the palm of his hand. As he glanced up, the smile slipped from his face, making his mother turn. Spotting Rob, she snatched her robe from the back of a chair.

Rob looked at the floor, but sensed her drawing near.

He saw stains on the carpet.

'Rob.'

The voice sounded faint, as if travelling through an underground tunnel.

She placed a finger beneath his chin, tilting it upwards. 'It's nothing. Do you understand?'

He noticed her eyes were bloodshot.

Edie McKenzie gripped his shoulders. 'Answer me.'

'Yes.'

The air smelt of cigarettes and sour milk. She smiled. 'So you can keep a secret?'

Rob nodded.

'Good.' His mother tried running her fingers through his hair, but he pulled away.

'Back to bed.'

He caught another glimpse of the stranger before the door closed.

As Rob walked down the hall, his chest remained tight. He stopped outside the living room and looked in. His father slept on the couch, while the lamp in the corner cast a sad yellow light.

Graves by the Sea

Standing at the top of the headland, Alex let the sea air fill his lungs. The sun hovered above the horizon, staining the ocean blood-red.

The church was positioned near the northern cliff's edge, surrounded by hundreds of lop-sided crosses blackened with age. To the building's left, a grove of pine trees dipped and swayed, speckling the cemetery with shadows.

Alex wandered through the graveyard, reading tombstones as he went, studying their age, along with the mildew that crept across grey lettering. He glanced towards the church and noticed its intricate cobbled brickwork. A white cross topped the steeple, bright with morning light.

He walked to the trees, sat in the shade and pulled the sketch book from his bag. Behind him the sea pounded the headland's face.

Viewing the church side-on, he captured line and depth, before turning his attention to detail. Attempting to do the arched windows justice, he lost track of time.

Eventually, Rose appeared in the graveyard. Moving through dappled sunlight, her long hair lashing

about, she looked ethereal, almost like a ghost.

He put the sketch book away and stood.

Rose stopped in front of him. 'Working already?'

'A little.'

'Told you there'd be something to draw.'

'It's a beautiful place.'

'You should see it at night.'

'Yeah?'

Rose began to follow a path into the thicket of trees and Alex trailed closely behind.

'I suppose it sounds scary, coming to a graveyard at night,' she said, 'but it's not. It's peaceful and quiet.'

Above them, branches trembled.

The grove thinned as they came to a wire fence, which was orange with rust and supported by rotting timber posts.

Rose climbed over it.

'What are you doing?' Alex asked.

'What's it look like?'

'Something crazy.'

'Come on,' she said. 'Just watch your step.'

Below, the ocean hummed.

Alex negotiated the fence, took a couple of steps and stopped beside Rose, who stood half a meter from the cliff. Before them, a blue plain of water stretched on forever.

Staring out to sea, Rose edged her way forward. 'Takes your breath away, huh.'

'Definitely.'

The promenade was wide so that the corners of its flanking bays remained hidden, tucked in on either side. This cliff was less steep than that which boasted the lighthouse at the southern end but, peering down, Alex saw protruding rocks and thin ledges. A fall would mean death. Below, the water rushed in, stopping short of the granite face before racing back.

Rose held out her arms and took another step, allowing her toe's to nudge the cliff's edge.

'What are you doing?'

'Learning to fly.'

He moved towards her. 'What?'

'Sometimes, when I stand here, it feels like I'm flying. Try it.'

Alex took hold of her arm. 'Rose.'

'What?'

'Step back.'

'Why?'

'It's dangerous.'

'Do you always worry so much?'

'Things happen.' He licked his lips. 'Accidents.'

She held his gaze, then slid past. 'Come on, Mr Safety Comes First, I want to show you something.'

They headed north, following the fence line.

'Where are we going?'

She pointed to the northern bay below, where the tide appeared to be going out. 'Down there.'

Loose stones slid beneath his shoes. 'How do you plan on getting there?'

'You'll see.'

'If you're going to scale down the cliff, I'll leave you to it. I'm not good at that sort of thing.'

'Relax. Everything will be fine.' Rose seemed to glide across the ground as she skirted the precipice.

As Alex followed, adrenaline flooded his veins. Spotting a cast iron gate in the fence, he said, 'Why didn't we just come through that?'

'Wouldn't have been as fun, would it?'

He stopped and stared at a set of stone stairs that had been carved into the cliff face. Below this, not far from the rocks, a shipwreck's rusted remains erupted out of wet sand.

'Great subject matter,' Alex said.

'Sure is around this town.'

'Sorry?'

'Nothing. Let's go.' Rose bowed her head and began descending towards the sea.

Alex followed. Reaching the base of the cliff, he eyed the broken vessel, which he guessed was around 36 feet long. The shallow water revealed a busted hull covered in barnacles.

Rose brushed against him, setting his skin alight.

'A fishing boat?' he said.

'Yep. Ran aground during a storm.'

'Maybe they should put a lighthouse here, too.'

'Bit late.'

The ocean licked at the wreckage.

'When did it happen?'

'Ten years ago. They never found the bodies.'

'Really?'

'Yeah.'

'Strange,' he said.

'Lots of strange things happen along this beach.'

'I almost drowned in the sea once.'

She looked at him. 'What happened?'

'Got caught in a rip and dragged out.'

'Sounds like you had a lucky escape.'

'Yeah.' He screened his eyes with a hand. 'Sometimes I wonder how close I came to death that day.'

'Who knows?'

'Maybe God.'

'You believe in God?'

'I used to. Now I'm not so sure.'

Rose picked up a shell and examined it. 'I don't.'

'No?'

'I only went to church because Dad wanted me to. These days he can't make it there.' She threw the shell into the water. 'Believing in stuff like that is taking the easy way out.'

'Why?'

'When we point to a higher power, to something supernatural, it helps us feel safe. But the truth is, there's no one looking out for us.'

'How did we get here, then?'

'I think it's random. Existence, the universe, everything. We're floating around on our own, for not much reason.'

'So it's all a matter of chance?'

'Yep, that's how I see it.'

'What about choices?'

'What about them?'

'Don't they make a difference to how we live, to what happens?'

Rose shrugged. 'Maybe, but do we really have choices, or do we just do what we need to?'

Alex didn't answer.

'The thing is, if you don't believe in some grand wizard making sure things go to plan, then you can't be disappointed.'

Alex stared down at the wreck. 'I guess not.'

Lizard Man

Rob struggled to his feet and looked about the empty landscape. The heat was relentless. He touched his lips, which were blistered and split. His tongue scraped the insides of his mouth as he tried to swallow.

How long had he been in this God forsaken place? Had it been days? Weeks? Shielding his eyes, he turned in a circle. Endless hills of corrugated sand were occasionally interrupted by tufts of grass. Out along the horizon, the desert kissed the sky. There wasn't another living soul in sight.

Several hundred meters to the west, a dune soared into the air, offering a sliver of shade. He staggered towards it, boots squeaking. Heat waves shimmered. Reaching the base of the dune, he dropped to his knees and wept. Grit scratched the underside of his eyelids. Rob swallowed hot air, held it in his lungs, then released it through his nose.

He'd reach the end of the line without a fuss.

But what was the point of maintaining his dignity if there was no one to witness it? He lay back, feeling the earth's warmth through his shirt, and tried to ignore the spasms in his bowel.

The sky looked like the sea and the sea was the desert in disguise. None of it could be trusted.

An eagle circled, a white glitch in the endless blue above. A memory surfaced and Rob saw his brother's hand slipping into the ocean. He struggled to retain the image, to remember what happened next, but failed.

His head spun; he propped himself onto an elbow and dry-reached. Looking back to the sky, his vision cleared.

What would take him first? Wild dogs? Birds of prey? Giant lizards?

What did it matter? He simply wanted it all to be over.

The muscles in his back contracted, forcing him to cry out. When the cramps passed, he felt himself sinking into the sand. Was he leaving his body? It was hard to tell. All he knew for certain was that he longed to moisten his lips.

A whirl of brightly colored lines swam through the air, sending his head into a spin. Closing his eyes, he rolled onto his side and imagined cool winds rising from the sea, tearing through mountainous borders, across barren plains to meet him.

Out of the blue came laughter that tumbled through the air, running up and over the dunes.

The sound morphed into a sphere of light, which sped away and came to a standstill in the distance; it hovered in the air, waiting. He watched as deep fissures appeared at the sphere's polar ends. The lines ran deep, until the entity of light split into two, then four. The lights morphed into horses, each mounted with a rider. Closer they came, hooves pounding, cloaks billowing. The riders would sweep down and steal his soul, leaving behind a bag of bones. He struggled to watch their approach, but his eyelids drooped. Spreading his limbs beneath the sun, Rob surrendered, letting the darkness take him.

When he came to, circles of white swarmed his vision. They swirled, shrank, fell into one another, then swelled again before contracting into a blur of brightness. What had happened to the cavalry of horsemen?

As his sight sharpened, Rob saw a single horrific entity close by.

The creature's body seemed human, but the head was reptilian — its nose and mouth resembled a turtle's beak and its skin was speckled with shiny scales. Inside its head, dark marble eyes swiveled. Clumps of grey hair sprouted from beneath its hat, which was rimmed with string and cork. It wore jeans and a red check shirt.

The lizard man knelt and opened his beak. A slab of intestinal-pink muscle, pointed to a tip, slipped out from behind sharp teeth and thrashed from side to side. Rob scrambled backwards, his elbows digging into the sand.

Raising a clawed hand, the creature spoke. Rob couldn't hear a word, but he saw the letters; they tumbled from the creature's mouth and bobbed in the air. He seized upon the fragmented signs and attempted to understand them.

Struggling to think in the searing heat, Rob felt a circuit blow inside his brain. The planet swung on its axis, the desert floor tilted, and clouds slid down the sky. A shower of sparks pierced his vision, before darkness came for him once more.

Rose's Place

Alex followed Rose along a dim corridor and past the kitchen, where he glimpsed a sink with a dripping tap. In the lounge, shards of sunlight seeped through metal blinds. The room contained an old stereo, a stack of albums, and a piano lined with framed photographs. Bright blankets were strewn across a couch near the window. A velvet-covered chair filled one corner of the room.

Rose made space on the couch, her back peeking out from beneath her shirt. When she'd finished, the blanket pile reached the window ledge. 'Sit down.'

Alex gestured towards the blankets. 'What are these?'

'Blankets — I made them.'

He raised a brow. 'Really?'

'Really.'

'You made *all* of them?'

'That's right.'

He sat beside her. 'How long did it take?'

'That bunch? Maybe two months.'

'What do you do with them?'

'Sell them at the markets. They're a hit in winter. I stockpile a little in the warmer months, as you can see.'

'Got any other hidden talents?'

'I wish.' She rested her feet on the coffee table, nudging aside a set of knitting needles attached to a bundle of wool. 'But I'm just a quiet country girl. No exciting secrets.'

'Who taught you how to knit?'

'Mum.' Sunlight slid across her cheek.

'You miss her?'

'Yeah, I do.'

'How old were you when she died?'

'Eight.'

The blind clanged against the windowsill.

'So where's your dad?'

'Sleeping. Early-onset Alzheimer's kicked in a few years ago.' She glanced at her watch. 'I'll wake him in a couple of hours, give him lunch. He often sleeps during the day, then lies awake at night. Sometimes I find him staring into the dark. I think that's when he remembers things and relives the past.'

Alex took hold of her hand. She lifted a finger and touched his lips. When he opened his mouth to speak, she leant forward and kissed him.

He rubbed the back of her hand with his thumb. 'I probably won't be in Pegasus for long.'

Rose rested her head against the couch and stared at the ceiling. 'Can't a girl have a little fun?'

'I guess so.'

'Good.' She picked up her knitting needles. 'Besides, it's nice to have company. There's hardly anyone to hang out with around here. Everybody leaves, heads for the city.'

'Everybody?'

'Mostly. I had a few friends at school, but they've gone now.'

'What about you?'

'What about me?'

'Will you head for the city, too?'

'Probably, but not yet.'

'What do you want to do?'

'I'm hoping to study fashion design.' Her fingers worked the wool — over, around, under.

'Is there a school for that kind of thing in Pegasus?'

'No, but it's okay. This is where I need to be for now.'

The sound of the sea drifted into the room.

'So how are those drawing lessons going?' she asked.

'Great. We mostly work at night.'

'I'm glad it's going well.' Rose put down the needles and got to her feet. 'You want some tea?'

'Sure.'

'Check out Dad's music collection if you want. It's ancient, but kind of interesting.' She disappeared through the doorway.

Alex heard water running, metal clanking, cupboards opening. He stepped forward to inspect the photographs on the piano: there was a baby girl holding a ball; a man and woman embracing in front of the house; and Rose, suddenly older, sitting beside the same man, her arm threaded through his.

He tried to imagine how alone Rose must have felt, especially given her father's worsening condition. His thoughts turned to his own father, still alive, but absent, missing in action. How much had his psychological disintegration damaged Edie McKenzie? How much must she have missed their former life together?

His mother had been unfaithful, even promiscuous, but she wasn't a bad person.

The kernel of anger inside Alex's chest softened as he returned to the couch. What else would the sad girl in the kitchen teach him?

The Crossing

Rob tried to swallow, but his mouth was bone dry; his head screamed with pain. The surrounding sand-coloured walls flapped and sighed. His eyes moved from left to right, up and down. He was lying on a hessian bed a few feet above the ground and a silver tarp covered the desert floor. A man wearing jeans and a check shirt stood nearby. The stranger was tall and thin, his long hair streaked grey.

Memories of a lizard man swam through Rob's mind. Had he been dreaming?

The man came closer, put a bottle to Rob's lips and held it still. Rob drank. The man then crossed to a table, placed down the bottle and sat in a decrepit folding chair.

'Who are you?' Rob's voice was hoarse.

'Gordon Brown. Found you about five K's from here, delirious.'

'I broke down. I don't know how long ago. Days, at least. Probably shouldn't have left the car.'

'You're lucky we crossed paths. It might not have turned out that way if you'd stayed put. The desert can kill a person faster than you'd believe.'

'I saw things, some sort of lizard man. He was dressed like you.'

Gordon crossed his legs. 'You'll see strange things out here — the sun, the heat — it plays tricks. Nothing's quite what it seems.'

'I'm Rob McKenzie.' Thank Christ he could remember his name.

'You're a lucky man, Rob. No I.D. on you. Don't know what I would've done if you'd died. Gone to the cops, I s'pose.'

'I had a camera.'

'Over there.' Gordon pointed to the table, which was covered with various tools, plastic containers, fragments of metal. The camera appeared to be in one piece.

The canvas walls shuddered.

Rob's head throbbed as he tried sitting up. He lay back and closed his eyes. 'Can I have more water?' The tarp crackled. A bottle was pressed to his lips and he drank. Images passed through his mind: a twisting brown river glinting with beads of light, an animal's legs laboring beneath him.

'How did we get here?'

Gordon sat down again. 'Camel.'

'Sorry?'

'By camel. I operate camel tours.' He shrugged. 'Not a bad way to make a living.'

'Get many customers?'

'Enough.'

'Who?'

'Couples on honeymoon, executives escaping the city, people trying to fix broken lives. Even came across a run-away once, young woman who'd given her husband the slip.'

'You work by yourself?'

'Yep.'

'Must get lonely as hell.' Rob could smell a story. He'd take a personal angle, depict a man who refused to be penned in, someone who stood alone against the elements. Gordon brown was cover story material.

'Sometimes. But, like I said, there's often people around. To tell the truth, they piss me off.' Taking what looked like a Swiss army knife from his pocket, he tested its blade against the hair on his forearm.

'Why?'

'Usually whinge too much.' Gordon shut the knife and slipped it into his shirt pocket. 'You gonna tell me what you're doing out here?'

'Shooting photos.' The words sounded ridiculous, even to himself.

'Of what?'

'The country.' Rob remembered driving into the desert. Why hadn't he turned back? His head spun and the nausea returned. 'I'm going to be sick.'

A bucket appeared beside him; Rob vomited water and bile. Sweat trickled from his temples. Gordon walked away, unzipped the tent and slipped into the darkness. The contents of Rob's stomach sloshed across the desert floor. Gordon reappeared, placed the bucket near the table, grabbed the water and stopped by the bed.

Rob cleared his throat. 'My head feels like it's about to explode.'

'You're dehydrated.' Gordon put the bottle to Rob's lips once more. 'Drink.'

Cool liquid slid down his throat. 'How long have I been here?'

'A few hours.' Gordon returned to his chair. 'We arrived on dusk.'

'Did we cross a river?'

'Yeah.'

'I remember seeing water.'

'What else?'

'An animal. We were riding on an animal.'

Gordon nodded. 'My camel.'

'Right.' Rob rubbed his forehead. Events were reassembling themselves — he remembered what happened in the cellar with Kieran and how Cal had left. Regret grew inside him like a tumor. 'I've been pretty mixed up since leaving Talinga.'

'What were you doing there?'

'Research. I'm a journalist.'

'Been sucked in by those spooky stories?'

Wind tugged at the walls.

'Maybe.'

'You believe everything you hear?'

'No.'

'That's good.'

'I don't know what to believe anymore. For all I know, you could be a figment of my imagination. No offense, but there's no trusting my brain these days.'

Gordon laughed. 'If I'm not real, then neither are you. Who do you write for, one of those glossy women's mags?'

Rob didn't answer.

'That stuff about Talinga is all Chinese whispers, son. Started off as a bit of a murder mystery — God knows how long ago — did a squillion turns through the rumor mill, gathering more melodrama as it went. Nobody knows what happened to Vanessa Clark and Albert Bowen. If you want my opinion, their carriage ditched into the creek and they died. Simple.'

'How come the bodies were never found?'

'It's a dark, murky place. They didn't have the technology we've got now.'

'What about the carriage?'

'Patterson Creek was deeper back then.'

'And the priest who jumped from the bell tower?'

'What about him?'

'I heard he died a year to the day after Vanessa and Albert went missing.'

'It's what you call a coincidence.'

Rob released a rush of air.

'What? You don't believe in coincidences?' Gordon said.

'Not always.'

'Okay, let me ask you this — where did you hear about the story?'

'On the Net.'

'I rest my case. You can't trust anything on there.'

'I got some information from the caretaker, too.'

Gordon shot him a glance. 'Kieran O'Brien?'

'You know him?'

'Sure. We've crossed paths. Strange bloke. Likes it both ways, so I've been told.' Gordon shrugged. 'Doesn't bother me. This place attracts all sorts. In any case, O'Brien keeps to himself. Seems no one really knows the man, so I'd never trust him.'

Listening to the wind, he thought of Alex, who was always on-line, chatting with imaginary friends. Floating through cyberspace was probably like being stuck out in the middle of nowhere — people could be whoever they wanted. Rob wished he'd told his little brother he could stand proud, that he was a great artist. Instead, he'd let him drown in self-doubt.

'Try to rest, son.'

He nodded and closed his eyes.

The Night

The sun squatted low in the sky, staining the horizon blood-red. Alex could hear the pulse of the sea as he wandered down the side of the church. Finding a side entrance, he stood in the doorway and let his eyes adjust. The air flickered with a golden glow. The church seemed larger than it appeared from outside. He imagined the building bulging, God's presence too much for its little seams, then his heart sank. When would he start to see things clearly?

Inside, it was quiet. A candle burnt on the altar. Behind this, light spilled through a stain-glass window and across the floorboards. Alex walked up the aisle, reached the front pew and stopped. The back wall featured a painting of Jesus in a storm at sea. The ocean surged and men lunged at windswept ropes, but Jesus looked calm.

Behind him a floorboard creaked. Alex turned and saw a man near the altar. Dressed in jeans and a polo shirt, he carried a book and wore a cross around his neck.

'I'm sorry,' the man said. 'I didn't mean to disturb you.'

'That's okay.'

'I'm Father Breen.'

'Alex.'

The men shook hands.

'Always a pleasure to welcome newcomers to the parish.'

'I'm just visiting.'

'What brings you to Pegasus?'

Alex looked around the church. 'The sea, I suppose.'

'That's as good a reason as any. Our coastline certainly is charming.'

'Dangerous, too.'

The priest nodded. 'Pegasus can be treacherous, with the sea working itself into a frenzy during storms. Much like you see in that picture.'

Alex turned to the painting. 'It's impressive.'

'It is.' Father Breen placed the book on the altar. 'It's also an apt visual representation for this part of the world.'

'What do you mean?'

'Around here the weather hits without warning. Storms roll in from nowhere. Keeps us on our toes.' Father Breen motioned to the front pew. 'Have a seat.'

Alex did as he was told.

'Where are you staying?'

'With Molly Knowles.'

'Do you share her love of art?'

'Yeah. How did you know?'

The priest smiled. 'Lucky guess.'

'Her son, Henry Knowles, is my doctor.'

'Is that right? I've known that boy since before he could walk.' He met Alex's gaze. 'Have you been ill?'

'Yeah.'

'What was the matter, if you don't mind me asking?'

'I had leukaemia a few years back.' He paused, then added, 'It recently led to some complications.'

'I'm sorry to hear it. Are you better now?'

'I hope so, but can't be sure.'

'Sounds like you've had a tough time.'

Alex thought for a moment; talking to a stranger left him feeling vulnerable, yet it brought comfort, too. 'Sometimes I wonder why it happened.'

'The leukaemia?'

'Yeah. I know about abnormal cell division and how it crams out healthy cells. The abnormalities are usually caused by some problem with the error-correction machinery inside cells. But why does that happen in the first place? That's what I don't understand. Is it just bad luck, or is there more to it?'

Father Breen shook his head. 'I don't know.'

'Nobody does. It's frustrating.'

'Some things defy explanation. What preceded the Big Bang, for instance? There must have been something, but we'll never know the answer until God chooses to reveal it. Even then, we may not understand.'

'You believe in the Big Bang?'

'Why not? The scenario doesn't discount God. On the contrary, it prompts us to question what happened before that miraculous event. What ignited the initial spark of life? I don't think science alone will ever get to the bottom of it.'

'And evolution?'

'The church is gradually coming to terms with Darwin's theory.'

'What do you believe?'

'I believe in both.'

'Really?'

'Is that so surprising?'

Alex shrugged. 'I guess not.'

'Much of the science behind Darwin's theories is irrefutable. As was the case with Galileo's work, despite his persecution. But again, the science doesn't displace God. Nothing does.'

'Nothing?'

'That's right.'

'But how do you know that?'

'Because the human soul was created by a higher power. That's why you're never alone, because He is within.'

'It doesn't seem like that sometimes. When you're sick, the fear crowds everything else out.'

'Only if you let it.'

Alex stared at the altar. A while ago, probably around the time of his relapse, a hole had grown inside him. He wasn't sure it could ever be filled, but how could he explain that to a priest? 'I don't seem to know what faith is anymore.'

'Sure you do,' Father Breen said. 'It's the bridge that keeps you connected with God.'

'In that case, I doubt I'll ever find it again.'

'Why?'

'I don't know, I just feel empty.'

'There were times when Jesus probably felt empty, too. And alone.' The priest put a hand on Alex's shoulder. 'But God has a plan for us all. When we except this, we step into a position of grace and more readily see signs of His presence. Then there's no need to be frightened.'

They sat in silence, the sound of the sea no more than a faint hum. On the altar, the candle's flame trembled.

Finally, Alex stood. 'I should be going now. Thanks for the chat, Father.'

'You're welcome. I hope to speak with you again sometime. Take care, now.'

'I will.' Alex left and stepped into the night, his path illuminated by the light of the moon.

Falling: A Dream

Rob stood on the edge of a cliff and looked out at a great expanse of desert. Spreading his arms and leaping forward, he felt no fear, only the rush of freedom. The wind rose to meet him and before long he was gliding high above the earth. An eagle appeared to his right, eyes glinting black and gold, its cry ripping through the quiet.

Rob drifted towards the bird, letting his fingertips brush against its wing. A flash of light flared inside his mind; when it had passed, things looked different. He'd entered the bird's mind. Or was the bird inside him? Either way, his field of consciousness had shifted.

Ribbons of pink light streaked the sky. Far below, an animal scurried for cover. Rob tracked its movements, then turned to look at the eagle, which was heading for the sun. He squinted against the glare as the bird sailed higher, its wings fluttering.

The sun rolled across the sky, leaving behind a blazing trail of white. Feathers rained down like small silver arrows and the eagle plummet-ed. The approaching figure transformed into a man, who rushed past, howling. Recognizing his own face, Rob saw himself hit the earth.

He lay motionless, a smudge against the orange sand.

Continuing to soar, Rob wondered when he'd reach the end of the world.

The sky was an endless blue, and the desert a bright, golden sea.

Secrets

Alex opened his eyes and stared at the ceiling. He felt a sudden urge to draw all over it — pictures of her, Kelly. He'd received a letter the previous day; it rested among medicine bottles on the bedside-table. Reaching over, he picked it up and read it again. She wrote about how she'd settled into her dorm at uni, explaining that she liked her roommate. She said she missed him.

Alex swung his legs over the edge of the bed before placing the letter back in position. The paper quivered. Unscrewing one of the medicine bottles, he took out a white pill, placed it in his mouth, and washed it down with water left from the night before.

He walked to the window and saw clouds covering the sky. If the rain held out, he'd head for the beach and draw the wreckage.

The ocean hummed in the distance, stirring memories of Eight Mile. He knew Rob remembered that day, although they'd never discussed it. Some things were best left in the past.

Alex missed his brother. Had he nailed his story? He'd spoken with his mother the other day, but she'd received no word from Rob. Presumably, he was busy working. Still, it didn't take much to pick up the phone.

He listened to the house groan; it was easy to imagine the walls talking to one another.

Alex was alone. The previous evening, Molly told him she was going out and he'd been looking forward to the solitude.

He picked up his bag, which was packed with drawing gear, grabbed his brother's cap and walked down the hall. Passing Molly's study, Alex stopped and looked in — there were drawings all over the walls. He crossed the threshold, moved towards the center of the room and turned full circle. The sketches were mostly of the sea, but there were portraits, too, the Doc as a kid, and an older man who looked like the Doc, probably his father.

Alex examined the walls; it was like staring into Molly's soul. Did she recognize her own talent?

A pile of drawings had been stacked on the desk. He sifted through them, noting they were all seascapes, except for one right at the bottom that showed the graveyard overlooking Pegasus. A full moon hovered above the church, spilling light over the building and surrounding tombstones. In the bottom left corner, a dark figure — almost otherworldly — was entering the scene.

Did Molly believe in ghosts?

He tidied the drawings, before inspecting the desk more closely. There were two drawers: the top contained sketching equipment and stationery; the bottom was filled with newspaper clippings, which he pulled out and spread across the desk. Images of Michael Knowles and Chelsea McGovern stared back at him. Another clipping showed Rose as a small child. There were no photographs of Molly. Various pictures of the Pegasus shipwreck captured the vessel's gradual deterioration.

Words and pictures assembled themselves, spilling out the truth.

Everybody in town must have known what happened that night, yet neither Molly nor Rose had mentioned a thing. Why?

Looking up, Alex saw Molly standing in the doorway, her expression blank.

He watched as she turned in silence and walked away.

Turning Back

When Rob walked outside, the sky was awash
with stars. Gordon sat before a campfire, while
flames licked at the darkness.

'You want something to eat?' Gordon looked
over his shoulder. 'There's oats or dried meat.'

'No, thanks. I still don't feel great.' Rob sat on
the ground, pulling his knees up to his chest. 'How
long have I been sleeping?'

'A couple of hours. You needed it.'

Gordon drank from a small metal canister, then
held it out. Rob took it; the liquid burned his throat
and rested hot in his stomach.

Camels stood nearby, their curved bodies soaking
up starlight. A mournful howl filled the quiet.

'What was that?' Rob said.

'A desert fox.'

Rob remembered the small animal he'd seen
back near the car. 'Do they bother you?'

'Nope. Never come close.'

'I guess they're company.'

'Well, they prove the place isn't desolate.'

A shooting star dragged its fiery tail across the
sky.

'I've seen some strange things the past few days,' Rob said.

Looking at Rob through narrowed eyes, Gordon took another swig of his drink.

'You ever seen anything weird out here?' Rob asked.

'Yep, shit loads of stuff — but it's probably my imagination. The desert's bent on tricking the mind.'

'So how do you know what's real?'

'Why does it matter?'

'I guess I'm scared.'

'Of what?'

Rob considered the question, then said, 'Madness — I get the feeling it's stalking me.'

Gordon shrugged. 'We all lose our minds at some point. Some of us more than others. It's no big deal.'

'The thing is, I saw aliens. They visited me,' Rob nodded towards the black expanse beyond the fire, 'out there.'

'Really? What did they say?'

'They asked if I'd go with them.'

'And?'

'I turned them down.'

'That's too bad. Could've been a blast.'

'The alien I spoke to — this little grey guy with a bulging head and slanted eyes — he gave me some kind of warning.'

'What did he say?'

'I can't remember. It's frustrating as hell.'

'You on drugs, son?'

'Not at the moment.'

'But you've taken stuff in the past?'

'I've dropped a couple of acid tabs. Had a few joints.'

The fire crackled.

'Did you eat anything out there?'

'Yeah, some white flowers.'

'Shaped like little bells?'

'Yeah.'

Gordon gave a low-pitched whistle. 'That explains it.'

'What?'

'You've been feasting on an hallucinogenic.'

'The flowers?'

'Yeah, the plant's called Pituri. It'll send you to the moon and back.'

'You think I was tripping?'

'I know it.'

'No, those aliens were real. They had a message for me.'

'What sort of message?'

'I told you, I can't remember. But I know what I saw.'

'No use me arguing. You've already made up your mind about things.'

Rob turned his gaze to the blazing stars that pierced the roof of the night.

'Look, I'll admit I've seen some weird lights in the sky, but they could be anything — air force, magnetic fields, spaceships.' He looked at Rob, his eyes shining in the fire's glow. 'Strangest of all are the lights that hover just above the ground. They're little orbs that flit about wherever they please.'

'Ghosts?'

'Could be, or maybe I'm just seeing things. Makes no difference anyway.'

'Don't you want to know the truth?'

'But, son, what is the truth? You gotta remember, people build their own little stories to make sense of things. Take Talinga — they see or hear things that can't be explained and say, "Oh, it's the wife's ghost clattering along in that carriage, she must've been out for revenge, the husband beat her so she found comfort in the arms of another, the wife tormented the priest and that's why he jumped." It never stops.'

'You think it's all bullshit?'

'I never said that.'

'Then what?'

'There are things we can't explain. Mysteries, you know? Some people can't accept that.'

Another howl sailed through the night.

'I need to get back to the homestead. All my gear's there.'

'I'll take you tomorrow.'

'You know how to get there?'

'Sure. That's the good thing about having been out here for years, I know my way around. A compass is mighty useful as well.'

'Thanks. I appreciate your help.'

'Don't mention it.'

They sat in silence, watching the fire burn.

As Rob stared into the flames, the alien's warning against turning back rushed to the surface of his mind. What did it mean? Was the creature saying he shouldn't return to Talinga? No, it couldn't have been that. Besides, his lap-top was there, his story. He had to return, if only for a few hours.

Rob considered sharing his recollection of the alien's warning, but decided against it — Gordon wouldn't have believed him anyway.

Trapped

Alex and Rose sat near the edge of the cliff, an expanse of silvery water stretching out before them. In the distance, an ocean-liner glided past, its cluster of golden lights drifting south. Behind them, the graveyard was silent.

A full moon floated in the sky.

'You see that buoy way off shore?' Rose pointed to a red light bobbing in the water. 'The one that's fitted with a bell?'

'Yeah.'

'Sometimes, late at night, even when the ocean is calm, the bell rings. Nobody knows why.'

'You ever heard it?'

'Only when the sea's rough. Never otherwise.'

'Who has, then?'

'Fishermen, mainly.' Rose sat with her legs bent, thighs cradled against her chest.

'Some people say the noise is made by souls who were lost at sea.'

'Ghosts?'

'I guess you could call them that.'

'And what do you believe?'

'I've never heard anything unusual.'

'That's not what I asked.'

'Sometimes I think I can hear something, but it could be my imagination.'

'Interesting story. My brother would love it.'

'Really?'

Alex nodded. 'Rob writes articles about all sorts of stuff. Right now he's in the desert researching a haunted homestead.'

'On his own?'

'No, his boyfriend went with him.'

'Must be great to chase your dreams. Can't see that happening for me anytime soon.'

'Why not?'

'It's not possible at the moment.' She looked towards the moon. 'Tell me something — do you envy your brother?'

Was he that easy to read? 'Why would I envy him?'

'For a start, it would be hard growing up with someone who knows exactly what they want out of life.'

'Yeah, ambition sucks.'

She laughed.

'I worry about him sometimes.'

'Why?'

'He gets so wound up.'

'You mean aggressive?'

'No, it's more like he fixates on making things happen. He's been like that since he was a kid. I'm scared one day it'll catch up with him.'

175

'What about your parents?' she said. 'Aren't they around?'

'Sort of.'

'Sort of?'

He didn't answer.

She leant forward and kissed him.

Alex ran a hand through her hair. 'You're real brave, you know that?'

'Me? Why?'

'Staying here and looking after your dad. It can't be easy.'

'I don't exactly have a choice.'

'There's always a choice.'

'Maybe. But sometimes life turns out a certain way and you just have to deal with it, you know?'

'Yep.' He let out a deep breath. 'There's something I've been meaning to tell you.'

She turned to him.

'I had cancer.'

'Really? What type?'

'It was leukaemia the first time, then a tumor appeared in one of my testes.' Alex picked up a rock and threw it over the cliff. 'That's why I'm here — to take it easy and hopefully get better.'

Rose kept quiet.

'It's all pretty heavy, I know.'

'I'm glad you told me.' She took hold of his hand. 'Are you okay now?'

'I think so.'

'It must have been tough, especially getting sick a second time.'

'Yeah.' Alex listened to the ocean, then said, 'Now it's your turn to share something.'

'My life's pretty boring — there's not much to tell you.'

'What about the fact your mother and Michael Knowles died together on that shipwreck?'

Rose shut her eyes. 'How did you find out?'

'I found some newspaper clippings hidden away in Molly's study.' She was quiet for a moment, then added, 'Why didn't you say anything?'

'I guess I'm ashamed.'

'You shouldn't be.'

'Easier said than done.'

'I suppose it is.' Alex put an arm around her shoulders.

'You know what gets to me the most?' she said.

'What?'

'Nobody really knows what happened, so people talk, making up stuff, and the rumors never go away. They're always there, just below the surface of every look, every conversation.'

'Have you spoken with Molly? Maybe she knows the real story?

'I tried — went around there once — but didn't get anywhere.' Rose put a hand to her mouth, then took it away. 'It's Dad I feel for the most. He was devastated when he heard about the affair. I'm hoping he's forgotten it all now.'

Below them, the sea thrummed.

'It's terrible when you can't protect the ones you love.'

Alex pulled her close. 'Yeah, I know.'

Ghosts

The homestead appeared to be empty. Rob arrived back at Talinga a few hours earlier, but was yet to cross paths with Kieran. Gordon had returned to his tent in the middle of nowhere. Rob planned on heading to the closest train station as soon as possible. Although, he had no idea how he was going to get there. In any case, for now he needed to work.

The computer's cursor blinked as words eluded him. Maybe the ghosts didn't want their stories told?

The homestead creaked and groaned. Glancing over his shoulder, Rob saw shadows sliding across the study walls. The lights went out and blackness engulfed him. Without even looking, he knew his lap-top had died. Why wasn't the battery kicking in?

In the corner of the room, the grandfather clock chimed.

He kept still, letting his vision adjust. A silvery light climbed through the window. Leaving the room, he moved into the corridor.

Strange sounds prodded his nerves. He heard a high-pitched electrical whine, then a low growl. It must have been his imagination running wild.

Rob spun around, his gaze groping at the dark.

He needed to head outside and check the electricity box. The problem was probably just a blown fuse. Rob grabbed a torch off the sideboard and headed for the front door; he gripped its handle, fingers clenched, and strained to listen.

A pool of light seeped across the threshold as he opened the door. It was brighter outside than he'd imagined and the sight brought him comfort.

Crossing the porch, he stopped at the stairs and looked up. A swollen moon hung in the sky, reminding him of his time in the desert, and he felt as vulnerable as a child.

Shame was a tight ball in his stomach. What grown man was scared of the night?

Walking down the stairs, he saw movement near the corner of the house. Rob stared into the gloom, then looked behind him. There was no one around. Gravel crunched beneath his boots as he walked. The homestead appeared to lean towards him while reflecting the moonlight. Turning at the edge of the house, he peered into the darkness that flanked its side. Something was down there. Red eyes gleamed, watching, waiting. Or was it the play of light?

Fear penetrated his limbs, weighing him down.

There was a flapping noise, then the beating of wings around his head. Rob recognized the outline of a black bird, its feathers shining like metal, then it was gone. He stood still, senses taut, but the red eyes had vanished.

Retracing his steps, he found himself back on the porch. Shadows lurked behind the front door. He remembered about checking the electricity box, but couldn't bring himself to go back.

Rob returned to the study, strode to the gun cabinet, took out a rifle and made sure it contained ammunition. With a gun in one hand and a torch in the other, he headed for his room.

In the morning, he'd phone for help. The sooner he went home, the better.

Forgetting

Alex pretended to study swirls in the table's grain,
while stealing glances at Rose. She stood with her
back to him, making coffee. He wanted to approach
her from behind, to slip his arms around her waist.
Could she sense it?

Sunshine poured through the kitchen window
above the sink. The tap released water droplets that
seemed ready to burst with light.

His brother's cap lay on a nearby bench,
forgotten.

Rose handed him a coffee and sat down, her
chin resting against the palm of her hand.

He gripped his cup. 'I meant what I said last
night.'

'We said a few things.'

'About you being brave.'

'If you only knew.'

'What?'

'I'm terrified of losing him.'

'Your dad?'

'Yeah.'

'I know what you mean.'

Outside, cicadas screeched in the afternoon heat.

'So what about your folks? You hardly mention them.'

'There's not much to say.'

'I don't believe you.'

Glancing towards the sink, Alex watched the tap drip.

'Well, I guess we're pretty even in terms of sharing secrets.'

'I guess so.'

Rose drummed her fingers on the table. 'You really want that coffee?'

He sat back, placing his hands on his thighs.

She stood, stepped forward, and pulled him to his feet. 'The way I see it, we've got to make the most of the time we have.'

'Sounds like a plan.'

Rose led him along the corridor that stretched towards the back of the house. She opened a door and closed it behind them.

It was a plain room with white walls and lace curtains. A double-bed had been positioned beneath a window. Against one of the walls leant a set of drawers, and upon them rested a sewing machine. A wooden chair faced the corner, its back draped with silky fabric. A dress-maker's model stood nearby, its naked limbs poised in mid-motion.

Alex walked towards the chair and rubbed the material between his fingers. 'No blankets?'

'Nope. This is where my real dreams live.'

He turned, watching as she took off her shirt, then her pants.

Rose stepped forward and placed her hands on his shoulders. 'Do I shock you?'

'No.'

She touched his ear with her lips. 'Liar.'

He slid his hands along her arms. 'What about your dad?'

Rose lifted his shirt, pulled it over his head, flung it aside. 'He sleeps this time of day. Always. Like a child.' She unbuttoned his jeans, slid them off, and led him to bed where they lay facing one another.

'You know," she said, 'I can see the stars from here at night.'

'Really?'

Yep. I've had burning rocks flying through my little part of the universe for years.' Lifting the curtain, Alex saw a vast stretch of blue. 'Ever make a wish?'

'Heaps, when I was little. Mum and I spent ages looking for blazing trails of light. I always made a wish when I spotted one.'

'What did you wish for?'

'All sorts of things. A new bike, dolls, an ant farm.'

'An ant farm?'

'Yeah. Weren't you ever interested in ants as a kid?'

'Can't say I was.'

'They're pretty amazing creatures. I'm sure they'd be great to draw.'

'I'll take your word for it.'

She laughed.

He kissed her.

'You ever done this before?' she said.

'What?'

'Slept with somebody.'

'A few times.'

'With different girls?'

'No, just the one.'

'What's her name?'

'Kelly.'

'Do you miss her?'

'Yeah.'

'But you're not together anymore?'

'Not right now, no.'

'Does that make you sad?'

'Sometimes, but I try not to think about it.' He ran a finger across her ribs. 'How about you? Is this something you're familiar with?'

'No, not at all.'

The curtains lifted and patches of sunlight crept onto the bed. Rose rested her arms above her head, crossing them at the wrists.

'You sure you want this?' he said.

'Yes.'

'I don't know how much longer I'll be in town.'

'It can't be helped.'

Alex slid a hand down her midriff. She smiled, trembling slightly beneath his touch.

Death at the Window

Rob lay on the bed, his breathing shallow; he'd been listening to strange noises for what seemed like hours. There was the dull clang of metal on concrete, like someone dragging chains.

Closing his eyes, he prayed.

He now believed the homestead was riddled with ghosts. Their presence seeped through the walls, instilling the house with an air of hopeless sorrow. They were angry, whoever they were. Christ only knew what they were capable of.

Outside, the wind howled.

Rob sat up and reached for the rifle, wrapping his fingers around the shaft. He fondled the cold metal, then rested the gun against the wall.

Darkness held him.

What if the whole place were to implode? Where would that leave him? Somewhere else, most likely. The idea seemed appealing.

The window rattled. Chains clinked.

There was a faint scream.

His skin was damp with sweat. Rob reached down beside the bed, grabbed the torch and switched it on. A thin ray of light struggled to penetrate the darkness. He approached the dressing table, looked into the mirror and froze. A man was seated in the wing chair in the corner of the room. Dressed in black, he sat looking towards the window. Staring at the reflection, Rob noticed the man's dark, deep-set eyes.

The torch faded. Rob looked at it, then back at the man, who seemed oblivious to his presence.

He spun around to face the chair, but saw nothing. Rob dragged his gaze up the walls, towards the ceiling, back to the corner. The figure had vanished.

Stepping forward, he stopped in the middle of the room and listened. Outside, the wind screamed. A cold draft swept over him, ruffling his hair. The window was shut — he was sure of it. He looked at the torch and watched the dim ray of light flicker, then disappear.

Rob's chest grew tight as darkness claimed the room.

What the hell was going on?

Nothing.

The word echoed inside his head. 'Who's there?' he said.

A bell rang out, deep and sonorous.

He began to tremble.

Again, the bell chimed.

He dropped the torch, fell to his knees, and placed his hands over his ears. On and on the bell clanged, its sound growing louder.

For the second time in his life, Rob prayed.

When he was certain he could no longer stand to listen, the bell stopped ringing. He sat on his haunches and took a shuddering breath. There was nothing to hear but the wind, the rattling window, the thudding of his heart. Rob crawled along the floor, reached the bed and climbed in. He longed for the solace of sleep.

The figure he'd seen in the mirror reappeared in his mind. It had been John Clark; those eyes were unmistakable. Had the ghost come from a world of in-betweens? And hadn't he wandered through a similar place while lost in the desert and close to death?

For some time, Rob cried. When he was done, he tuned into a strange noise, like shovels being dragged across the earth.

The noise grew louder. What was it? The realization struck hard and fast, crunching gravel.

The carriage of Talinga was coming.

The sound of approaching hooves shook the air.

He imagined the sight of the vehicle. Faintly lit and drawn by sleek black horses, it would float several feet above the ground. The ghosts would be inside, faint and trembling, trapped in no man's land.

What was he supposed to do?

How would John Clark's ghost react to the intrusion? The window rattled.

Sadness swamped him as he tried, but failed, to recall the faces of those whom he loved. Things would never be the same. Without memories, he was nobody.

He listened as the carriage drew up outside the homestead. Grabbing the rifle, he walked to the window.

Shadows danced.

Rob watched and waited.

A tall, silhouetted figure appeared behind the glass. A current of fear sped through his body.

He raised the rifle, rested the butt against his shoulder and squeezed the trigger. There was a blast, then he was flat on his back. Rob got to his feet, staring at the shattered window and gaping hole in the wall. Raising a hand, he found a shard of glass embedded in his cheek. He pulled it out, allowing blood to trickle down his face.

Curtains twisted in the wind.

He stepped through the hole and into the night.

A body lay on the porch, crumpled and bleeding. Rob stared, his breathing shallow, senses strung tight.

It wasn't meant to be this way. There had been a ghost. Now there was a body. Nothing made sense.

He heard the voice again.

Move Closer.

'What did you say?' he asked aloud.

There was no answer.

Glass crunched beneath Rob's boots as he walked. Then the bell began to toll once more.

He moved slowly, like an astronaut on a strange planet. The stars were going out and distant mountains glowed pink.

You could have him at least once more. Nobody would know.

Rob gripped his knees, turned and vomited, the contents of his stomach splashing across the floorboards.

The bell rang on.

In the distance, the wind whipped up monstrous waves of dust.

But there wasn't a carriage to be seen. Instead, there was a Ute parked nearby. The car seemed familiar.

He looked down at the body.

A stain, dark as ink, seeped across the floorboards.

Look at the mess you've made.

Rob knelt near the body, pushing the legs together and tucking the arms in close to the torso. Then he lay down beside the dead man and listened to the bell toll.

Tunnel Vision: A Memory

Miss Jennings looked up, pen poised. 'Having any bad dreams lately?'

'Just that one I mentioned last time.'

'Where you're in the tunnel of light?' Alex nodded.

'You had it again?'

'Yeah, last night.'

He'd had the same dream more times than he could count.

Miss Jennings scribbled in her notebook. 'How did you deal with it when you woke?'

'Wrote some poems.'

'Really? I never knew you wrote poetry.'

'It's not fit for public consumption.'

'I might think differently.'

'I doubt it.'

She smiled. 'So, what do you think this dream's about?'

'Maybe it's a warning.'

'About what?'

'Dying.'

'What makes you say that?'

He shrugged. 'I get this strange feeling when I have the dream.'

'What sort of feeling?'

'Like I'm drowning.'

'How do you know what that feels like?'

Alex considered telling her about the day he almost drowned, and the tunnel he'd seen as he struggled to stay alive, but the moment passed. 'Just a hunch.'

Miss Jennings shook her head. 'I don't think you're going to die anytime soon.'

'I never said it was me dying.'

'You think the dream's about someone else?'

'Maybe.'

'Alex, dreams allow our fears and desires to break out of the unconscious mind. Perhaps they're a coping mechanism designed to help us work through certain issues or problems. Some people think they're nothing more than random electrical impulses. The important thing for you to remember is that they're not real.'

He rubbed his knees. 'Right.'

'The drugs you're on at the moment are very strong. They stimulate the imagination.'

That was probably it.

'You should channel that energy into your drawings. Try to relax, okay?'

'Sure, I'll try.' Alex spoke the words without conviction. Nobody understood how realistic his dreams seemed.

Disintegration

The body was pale, its eyes shut. Rob got to his feet. A gash of sunlight bled across the horizon. Nearby, a Ute glistened with dew.

His thoughts were shards of broken glass. The voice commanded his attention:

Get rid of the body.

He didn't bother speaking aloud. *You want me to bury it?*

No time. Burn it.

Rob sobbed as he put a hand to his mouth. How had this happened?

He approached the corpse. Bending down, he grabbed the dead man beneath the shoulders and lifted; the body slumped forward, releasing a belch. Rob stopped and closed his eyes, breathing deeply. Lungs inflating, he saw oxygen rush into his alveoli and pass over into a network of tiny pink vessels. The vision settled him.

He dragged the body along the porch, down the stairs and across the dirt, his gaze fixed upon the dead man's shoes.

Rob stopped to adjust his grip.

Keep going.

He continued down alongside the homestead. Reaching the pile of timber near the shed, he rested the corpse on the ground. His heart felt ready to burst.

Up at the bell tower, a figure passed by the gap that was its makeshift window. Ghosts were watching — he'd deal with them later.

Rob tried dragging the body up the side of the timber pile, but slipped. Branches snapped as he fell, stabbing into his back. Pushing through the pain, he noticed the sky was a deep, clear blue. He strained to lift the body aside, then listened intently.

The bell had stopped.

Scrambling to his feet, he ran to the shed and grabbed a jerry-can of fuel. Rob threw petrol on the timber, doused the corpse and tossed the can aside. The homestead crouched nearby, watching.

Reaching inside the dead man's shirt, Rob took out a lighter. He lit a shaft of bracken and circled the pyre, setting its base alight.

The fire hissed as it consumed the corpse.

He slumped to the ground and lay back, his limbs spread wide.

Set the house alight. Burn them all.

Fuck you. I'm done.

The flames roared and the smell of burning flesh filled the air.

Beneath the crackling, he heard a steady, low hum. Vibrations ran through the earth and up into his back.

The humming grew louder. The ground trembled. The whir and thump of machines filled his head.

God, let it be over.

A terrible weight pressed against his chest. Maybe the devil had claimed him.

'Please,' he said, speaking with his eyes shut tight, 'take me away.'

Rob heard the sound of giant wings beating about his head as he slipped from consciousness.

The Vision

Alex lay in his bed at Molly's, straining to listen to the noises of the night. He'd been woken by something tapping against the window.

Moonlight flooded the room. The window rattled.

Outside, the ocean roared.

His breathing broke into gasps. A luminous figure hovered in the corner of the room, apparently waiting for something.

Alex sat up, his eyes wide open. The figure stared back.

Perhaps he was dreaming. Or maybe he was experiencing a flashback from the drugs he'd taken in hospital.

The figure was a flowing stream of light that floated several feet above the ground. Its face had once belonged to Cal.

So the man was dead. What about Rob?

The ghost responded, although its lips didn't move.

Not so good. He's pretty shaken up.

An image flashed through Alex's mind. His brother slept on bare earth beneath a dawn-pink sky. Nearby, flames roared.

Your brother's in trouble, but it was an accident.

Alex shook his head, trying to understand.

He didn't mean it. The ghost drifted towards the window. *Whatever happens, remember that.*

The figure began to fade. Or was it merging with the moonlight?

'Why have you come?' Alex asked.

Consider it a warning. You'll need to be strong.

The words sounded distorted, as if slipping through static.

The room seemed to grow brighter, then the ghost vanished.

Alex raced to the window and pushed it open. Wind lashed at his face as clouds skated towards the moon.

The ocean's scent hung in the air.

A high-pitched cry pierced the night. He turned and saw a bird in a nearby tree, its feathers glinting like metal. The creature cawed and tilted its head, staring with beady eyes. A veil of grey slipped across the moon and the bird disappeared.

Closing the window, he crossed the room and flicked on the lamp with trembling fingers. The lamp threw a soft yellow light, offering some comfort.

Alex's sketch book and pencil lay on the dressing table. As he reached for them, his legs crumpled and he fell to the floor.

Hell: A Dream

There was ice all around and it shone with a flickering orange light, as if reflecting unseen flames. A terrible cold bit into Rob's skin. Lifting his hands, he inspected his fingertips, which had turned black.

Despite the freezing temperature, the air smelt of burning flesh. The whir and thump of machines filled his head.

Had the Grim Reaper finally claimed him?

Where were the super heroes when he needed them?

He stepped forward and slipped, falling onto his knees. Peering through the frozen surface, Rob saw countless tortured souls below, their faces etched with horror. He pulled away, gasping, and struggled to his feet. Arms spread wide, legs bent, he turned around. Towering rock walls surrounded him. Overhead, the sky was dark. When he'd nearly completed a full circle, he saw a giant winged beast crouching in the shadows. It watched Rob with dark, miserable eyes. The creature exposed sharp yellow teeth as it shrieked.

Rob covered his ears and stepped back.

The beast stretched its wings, then tucked them away. Its hind legs were tethered by chains anchored in the ice.

'Who the fuck are you?' the creature said.

Rob said nothing.

'Cat got your tongue?' Sitting back on its rear end, cloven feet protruding at odd angles, the beast stared, its gaze burning with hatred. Apart from its wings and two small horns sprouting from its head, the upper half of the creature looked human. Its beard was thick and tangled; black coils of hair covered its muscular chest and arms. The lower part of its body resembled that of a goat.

'What's wrong?' it said. 'Not expecting me?'

'I don't know where I am, but there's been some kind of mistake,' Rob said.

'A little late to feign innocence, isn't it?'

'But I haven't done anything wrong.'

The beast screeched with laughter. 'People are so predictable. I can't tell you how often I've sat here listening to self-indulgent soliloquies — "I didn't do it. I was set up. The voices in my head got to me" — blah, blah, fucking blah. Frankly, denial bores me to death. Pardon the pun.'

'Who are you?'

Not real bright are you, sunshine?' The creature raised a thick brow. 'All right, let me spell it out for you.'

Dark letters tumbled from the creature's mouth, sliding across the ice: Rob recognized the word "Lucifer". None of this could have been real; he must have been hallucinating again. Looking at the walls, Rob shivered. There had to be a way out.

'Don't sweat it,' Lucifer said. 'You'll be here for a while yet. He'll let you suffer before offering redemption, but it's a better deal than I have. I'm here for all eternity.'

'I'm in hell?'

'My hell, actually. Who knows how many variations of the place exist. Apparently, this is the most dismal. You must have screwed up badly to end up here. Then again,' Lucifer rattled his chains, 'he's a tough task-master, awfully cruel.'

'God did this to you?'

The beast nodded, his pitiful eyes catching the light.

'What's He like?'

'Wouldn't you like to know?'

Rob waited.

'I could tell you. I could reveal all, in return for a small favor.'

'What sort of favor?'

'Release me, break my chains.'

'I can't.'

'But you don't know what it's like being stuck down here. It's awful. Torturous.' The beast dipped its head and sobbed.

'No.'

'Then stay. Please.' Lucifer jumped up, his hooves scraping at the ice. 'Everyone leaves me. I don't want to be alone.'

'I'm sorry. I can't help you.'

Lucifer's roar shook the air. 'Come here. I'll eat your fucking soul, suck it right out of you.'

Rob stumbled backwards.

'I can see your future.' The beast spat as he spoke. 'There's no hope. No hope at all. You're doomed to rot in your own despair. Then you'll be mine.'

The ground at Rob's feet split open, driving his legs apart. He fell backwards into frozen slush. There was a blinding flash of white behind his eyes, then he was numb, floating alone through an expanse of nothingness.

The End of the Line

On the edge of the graveyard, Alex and Rose sat facing the church. In the light of late afternoon, the scene looked impossibly beautiful; sky and sea seemed to merge. They'd been watching the sun sink for nearly an hour. Alex's insides were a tangled mess and it was time to come clean.

'Mum called me last night,' he said.

'How is she?'

'Not good.'

'What's up?'

'Rob's in trouble.'

'What do you mean?'

'He's been arrested.' Alex picked a blade of grass. 'He shot someone.'

She leant forward. 'Who?'

'His boyfriend.'

'Is he okay?'

Alex shook his head. 'Cal's dead.'

'Jesus.' She put a hand to her mouth.

'Apparently Rob was pretty messed up when the police found him. He was raving about being tricked by some ghost.' Alex remembered the vision he'd experienced the night before, but decided against mentioning it.

'Where did it happen?'

'At the homestead I told you about.'

'Out in the desert?'

'Yeah.'

'God, that's horrible. So, what now?'

'I don't know. The police took him into the nearest station. Mum's driving out there.'

'What about your dad?'

He scanned the graveyard, watching as trees swayed in the breeze. How could he explain that his own sickness had somehow shut Brian McKenzie down, pushed him over the edge? 'I don't have a typical family.'

Rose pushed hair away from his face. 'Who does?'

'Let's just say Dad lost the plot a couple of years ago. And Mum...she does the best she can.'

Rose kept quiet.

'I've been so worried about the cancer rearing its head again, I never expected anything like this to happen.'

'You couldn't have seen it coming.'

Alex shrugged.

'You want to be alone?'

'Not really.'

'Me neither.' She leant against his shoulder. 'What are you going to do?'

'I want to pretend Rob's fine, to travel along the coast and paint. Maybe sell my art.' He paused. 'But I need to go home.'

'Then that's what you should do.'

'I didn't think things here would end so soon. I thought I'd be here for a while longer.'

She kissed his cheek. 'Nothing lasts forever.'

'I guess not.'

'I won't forget you,' she said.

'Ditto.'

Past the church and beyond the cliffs, the ocean twitched with the day's remaining light.

Confession

Shouts rang out across the prison grounds. A basketball thumped on the court. Men jostled and jumped.

The sun shone.

Rob leant against the wall and looked up at an endless stretch of blue. The metal bench was cold beneath his legs.

Beside him, Father Brindley, the local priest, repositioned the book resting in his lap. 'It can be difficult to adjust to the confines of prison,' he said. 'You're doing well.'

'I'm no longer lost, Father. I feel close to God — it helps.'

'Yes.'

'I'd like to make a confession.'

'Certainly.'

Rob stared at the concrete. He remembered a time when the sun had scorched the earth, when there was nothing but sand as far as the eye could see, then the memory was gone. 'I've done some terrible things.'

The priest listened.

'I killed a man. I can't be sure of where, or how — because I struggle to remember things these days — but I know it happened.'

'Yes.'

'It was an accident.' He held the priest's gaze. 'But it was wrong.'

'Remember, He forgives all.'

Rob nodded.

Flipping through his book, Father Brindley stopped and opened it, 'Do you know Our Lady's prayer?'

'No.'

'Here.' The priest pointed to the top of the page. 'Let's say it together.'

Words quivered upon the page as Rob's eyes filled with tears.

Flames

They'd been tearing down the highway for an hour or so when Alex noticed a strange orange glow in the distance. He said nothing to Molly, who kept her gaze fixed on the road. Disappointment had been leaking out of her since the incident in the study; now it had crawled onto the seat between them, as inexorable as it was invisible. Night pressed against the windows. Wipers rubbed at the glass, pushing aside soft rain.

It seemed like months since he'd first travelled down this road. Somewhere along the way, time had twisted and wound back on itself, until there were no beginnings or ends, just a blur of events. What had that twisted passage of existence done to his brother? He imagined Rob sitting in a prison cell, his back to the wall, gloom wrapped around his shoulders.

The truck sped along the highway, hugging a corner. The scene they came upon was a blow to the senses. A hundred meters ahead, flames as tall as trees leapt into the air, devouring the darkness. Plumes of smoke spewed into the night, forming bulbous clouds tainted a bitter brown. The tyres tore up dirt as Molly pulled over. She killed the engine, leant forward and peered through the windscreen. 'Jesus Goddamn Christ.'

Alex wound down the window. The shape of a car flickered deep within the furnace, its metal gleaming white-hot. The air reeked of petrol and burning rubber. Fluorescent sparks floated through the air, disconcertingly beautiful.

Molly opened the driver's door, then looked back over her shoulder. 'Stay here.'

The rain had stopped, but streaks of water ran down the glass, distorting the light.

She stood in the fire's glow, a shivering silhouette.

Alex jumped from the truck and walked into a wave of heat.

When Molly spoke, her voice lacked certitude. 'Thought I told you to stay in the car.'

'What do you think happened? Alex asked.

'No idea.'

On the gravel verge, the flaming wreckage growled.

Alex stared at the fire. It could have been him and Molly in there; the truck could have slid out of control, slammed into a pole, burst into flames. In the space it took to take a breath, their lives could have ended.

How many times did a person cheat death without knowing?

'We've got to go,' Molly said.

They turned and walked to the vehicle.

'You think anybody was in there?'

She stared across the hood of the truck, her arms resting on the driver's door. 'I doubt it. Sure seems weird, though, coming across this with no sign of anyone around.'

'Maybe somebody's already stopped and helped, given them a lift to hospital or whatever.'

'Maybe.'

She slipped into the vehicle and Alex followed suit.

'We're we going?' he said.

'To the nearest phone.'

'You calling the cops?'

'Yep.'

Molly started the dual-cab and swung onto the bitumen. In the side mirror, Alex caught sight of the blaze, violent and bright. They rounded a corner and the flames disappeared.

'The car's probably been stolen, then torched. The Bay's got its dark side, like everything else — but I guess you already figured that out.'

He kept his mouth shut

They pushed on into the night, the roar of the engine blending with the hum of the road.

'I'm sorry,' she said.

'For what?'

'Giving you a hard time.'

'I deserve it.'

'Granted, you shouldn't have been snooping around my study but, the reality, is I'm just pissed off with the world. I've felt that way ever since I found out my husband was cheating on me.'

He gave a nod.

'You know, Henry and I never talk about what happened.'

'Do you want to talk about it?'

'Not really. As far as I'm concerned, it's ancient history. But sometimes I wonder if Henry blames me a little for how things ended up.'

'Why would he do that?'

Molly shrugged. 'Maybe I wasn't the wife I was supposed to be.'

'Nobody's perfect.'

'True.'

'I know what you mean, though — if only we could go back in time and change stuff, do things differently.'

'Yeah, if only.' Molly had expressed concern for Rob before they'd left and now she mentioned him again. 'I'm real sorry about your brother. I hope things work out for him.'

'Yeah, me too.'

They fell silent as through the windscreen darkness rushed towards them.

Chains

Rob sat on his bed, a notebook pressed against his thighs, and studied a crack running from floor to ceiling in the brick wall opposite; he scrawled another sentence. That crack lubricated his creativity, prompting him to stretch the boundaries of his mind. Writer's block wasn't a problem, but resources were limited. He didn't know when he'd be given more writing equipment. When he'd first asked for stationery items, the guard said many prisoners were denied such a privilege on account of the fact that it was hard to tell what someone might do with them. Evidently, the powers that be had decided Rob could be trusted with a pencil.

He chewed his bottom lip and looked around. The room was small with dirty white walls. There was a single steel-framed bed, a toilet and basin, a metal door locked tight.

His pencil scratched at the paper.

Moments later, Rob looked towards the barred window. Outside, the last throws of daylight stained the sky with pretty hues. He shut his eyes; certain stimuli brought to mind things he'd rather forget.

All that blood.

That beautiful face.

Flames consuming the night.

The images were difficult to shake once they'd struck and often looped mercilessly through his head. Then there was the distant tolling of bells, another unwanted distraction.

Fragmented memories drifted through Rob's mind, but he pushed them aside and forced himself to concentrate. Time was of the essence because soon the horsemen would come to take him away. He'd received this information from spirit guides responsible for guarding the gates between this life and the next; they often tapped into his psyche.

When he was done with his work, he'd be ready to leave.

Scribbling in his notebook, he watched letters skid across the page, then smiled as he finished a scene. The whole story had recently come to him in a dream; it had been crystal clear from beginning to end, a gift from God.

Set in an outback homestead that contained a labyrinth of rooms and hallways, his novel would convey a ghost story that explored the edges of psychological disintegration. Rob even knew how his fictional ghosts had died — a carriage had plunged into the deep waters of a local creek, drowning its two occupants, a woman and her driver. They were restless souls who longed for a proper burial.

The plot could have been that straight forward, but he'd drop hints of infidelity, suggesting foul play at the hands of an enraged husband. Ambiguity would intensify the story's sense of intrigue. And there'd be a suicidal priest who'd jump from the bell tower for reasons unexplained. Readers would wonder whether he'd been tormented by ghosts, or simply lost his mind? Rob also liked the idea of a maid kept in chains; she'd be the story's first and foremost spectra. The characters were fictional, yet seemed strangely familiar, as if they comprised some long forgotten part of himself. But what did it matter if the story were real or not? These days everything was a copy of a copy of something. True originality was a myth.

Rob looked towards the window. Behind the bars, silhouetted against the sky, a figure appeared. It had a thin face, slightly hooked nose and blue eyes. Rob saw the ghost repeatedly, day and night. He waited for it to speak, or communicate in some way. As always, the ghost stared straight through him.

What did it want?

The sound of rattling keys broke the silence and the ghost vanished. A guard opened the door. 'Visitors.'

Placing his notebook and pencil on the bed, Rob stood and stepped forward.

Home

From the front steps, Alex watched slabs of sunlight shift across the garden. His sketch book lay closed behind him on the porch. The sound of laughter floated in the air. Through the front gate, he spotted a couple of boys playing football on the street. He walked along the concrete path, stopped, and leant against the fence. One of the boys looked at him and waved. Alex lifted a hand in response. The same boy turned his face skyward and held out his hands, keeping his gaze glued to the ball. He caught it and grinned, booting it back down the street. The image grafted itself onto Alex's memory.

He often mentally photographed scenes. Details concerning the subject, light and mood were stored inside his brain, before being recorded through the strokes of a pencil. But Rob was the real photographer; his photos of the homestead out west revealed a place at odds with the world, its lines stark and jagged against a gaping sky. The desert images were some of the most haunting Alex had ever seen, while the recent pictures of Cal tore his soul. Then there were the photos of the caretaker, whose presence seemed cold, almost maleficent. How could that be captured through the lens of a camera?

Alex's train of thought was skittled when he saw Kelly walking up the street.

She caught his eye and stopped.

They stared at one another.

'You going to say something?'

He smiled. 'Hi.'

'Good to see you.'

'You, too.' Alex kicked a rock. 'You haven't started uni?' This wasn't what he wanted to say. He longed to tell her how much he'd missed her.

'Not yet. Classes begin next week.'

'Right.'

'I heard about what happened.' Her hair lifted in the breeze. 'I'm so sorry.'

'Who told you?'

'Mum. I came straight away.'

'Cal's funeral is tomorrow.'

'I know. It's tragic. He was such a beautiful guy. How are your parents?'

He shrugged. 'Dad looked straight through me when I told him. I wasn't sure if he heard, so I repeated everything. Then he cried.'

'So he understands?'

'I think so. Makes me wonder what things would be like if I could get through more often, connect with him, you know?'

'You miss him, don't you.'

'Yeah.' He watched the ball sail past.

'And your mum?' Kelly said. 'How is she?'

'She won't talk about it.'

'A lot's happened. She needs time to process things.'

'We went and saw Patricia Taylor yesterday.'

'And?'

'She's heartbroken.'

'I feel so bad for her.' Kelly turned towards the sky. 'And what about you? How are you holding up?'

'Okay.'

'You look well.'

'Thanks, I feel good.'

'Have you seen the doctor since you've been back?'

'No. I've got an appointment next week.'

'You're going to be fine.' More laughter came from the street. 'What will you do when you're given the all clear?'

'Hang here, I guess, and make sure everyone's okay.'

'You're staying in Sherbrooke?'

'Only for a while — it's time I got my act together and enrolled in art school.'

'Where will you go?

Alex turned to face her. 'I was thinking of heading north and cramping your style a little.'

'I'd like that.'

'I'll have to come back to see Mum and Dad pretty regularly, though. And then there's Rob...'

Kelly reached for his hand. 'How is he?'

'In some ways, he's the same — creative and energetic, fearless. In others, he's a complete stranger and I don't know if I can reach him.'

'Maybe things will get better with time.'

'Maybe.'

'I'd like to visit him before I head back. Could you take me?'

'Sure.' He kissed her.

'Did you draw while you were away?'

'Yeah, heaps.'

'Can I see?'

He stroked her hair, turned and headed towards the house. Kelly followed.

They sat at the top of the stairs. He grabbed his sketch book, then handed it over. Kelly turned the pages, then stopped. Instinctively, he knew she'd found the nude portrait of Rose. She closed the book, letting it rest on her lap. 'You seem to know her body very well.'

He said nothing.

'She's beautiful.'

'Yes.'

'Who is she?'

'A girl from Pegasus Bay.'

'Did you sleep with her?'

'Yeah, I did.'

'Do you love her?'

'We weren't together long enough for things to become that serious, but I'd be lying if I said I didn't care.'

'Are you going to see her again?'

'No.'

'I hate her anyway.'

'I'd hate anyone you got with, too.'

Birds sang, their sounds filling the quiet.

'When are you leaving town?' he asked.

'In a few days.'

'Well, I won't be far behind.'

'I'm glad.'

'I missed you,' he said.

'I missed you, too.' She met his gaze. 'I want you to draw me.'

'What did you say?'

'Draw me the way you drew her.'

'That's what you want?'

'Yeah.'

'All right.' Alex helped Kelly to her feet and led her inside.

Redemption

The cell was dark. Rob lay on his bed, listening to the sounds of human existence. Someone coughed, a voice called out, a guard yelled out instructions.

Closing his eyes, he let his muscles relax. As his thoughts settled, his mind became a blank screen. Rob felt his spirit rise up through the confines of his flesh before breaking free. His clothes hung loose on his silver-white body. He looked down at himself sleeping, then floated out through the barred window.

The ability to leave behind his physical body was proof God existed; his spirit would live on, life was eternal.

He flew across the basketball courts, down past the grassed area where prisoners exercised, out over the razor wire, and beyond to the river. It was a familiar journey, one he'd undertaken on two previous occasions.

The night was cool and clear. A full moon floated in space.

Drifting down through a stand of trees, Rob came to rest on the river's damp banks. Moonlight spilled across the water.

There was no nearby houses, no suburban lights.

Rob breathed in the quiet as wind swept through the trees.

He sensed the ghost before he'd seen it. 'I've finally figured out who you are.'

The ghost didn't answer.

'There's so much I don't understand, so much I forget when I'm back there.' He turned to look at the spectra, who had once been Cal. 'Here, it's different. Things make sense.'

'I know what you mean.'

'You're not wearing glasses.'

'Seems I don't need them anymore.'

'I suppose not.' Rob wiped his eyes. 'I never meant to hurt you.'

'I know.'

'I'm sorry I was such a prick.'

'That's all right. I loved you anyway.'

'Are you trapped?' Rob said.

'No, just in limbo.'

'What does that mean?'

'A few things need to sorted, but it shouldn't be long now.'

'Good — I'd hate to think you were lost between worlds.'

'It's nothing that bad. Besides, it's interesting being on the fringe of things. You'd love it.'

'Really?'

'Yep. There's plenty to write about.' The wind lifted, swirling around them.

'I got lost in the desert, Cal. That's when things first fell apart.'

'I know.'

'How could you?'

'In this world, there's no past or future. Time exists as a continuous stream and you can tap into events wherever you want. Consciousness becomes boundless. Cool, huh?'

'Sure. Unless there's stuff you don't want to know.'

Cal shrugged. 'Everything's how it should be.'

'Do you mean it all comes down to fate? That we can't change how things will be?'

'No, just that everything happens for a reason. It's universal law.'

Rob looked out at the slab of silvery water. 'There's something I want to know.'

'What?'

'Does God exist?'

A smile crept across Cal's face. 'I can't answer that.'

'Why not?'

'More universal law. There are codes, rules to be followed. I'm not even supposed to be here talking with you.'

'Then why did you come?'

'To let you know I'm okay.'

'Will you come back?'

'I don't think so.'

Rob looked at the burning stars, then turned to find Cal had gone. He stared out at the river, watching as splinters of moonlight danced across its surface.

The Visit

The visiting room was split in two by a brick wall and panels of bullet-proof glass. Physical contact between prisoners and visitors was forbidden. Alex and his mother shared a booth and a phone, their chairs pushed close together. Behind the square window, Rob sat with the phone to his ear. Edie McKenzie was doing most of the talking, her voice brimming with forced cheer.

'They treating you okay, Rob?'

Alex watched his brother's lips move.

Beside him, his mother smiled, but her eyes glistened. 'That's good. You look well.'

Rob spoke into the receiver again, his brow furrowed.

Edie McKenzie nodded. 'You still writing that story you told us about last time?'

As Rob replied, Alex studied his face; he was gaunt, his eyes feverish and bright. A lump formed in Alex's throat and he forced it down.

'That's great, honey. You've got so much talent. Remember that, okay?'

Rob nodded.

'Your brother wants to say hello. I'll put him on.'

Alex placed the receiver against his ear. 'Hey, how you doing?'

'Good. You?'

'I'm okay.'

'You still drawing?' Rob asked.

'Yeah.'

'You're really good. You know that, right?'

'Thanks.'

'I should have told you that a long time ago.'

'Don't worry about it.'

Rob licked his lips. 'Look, I need to get a move on with things.'

'What do you mean?'

'They say my time's nearly up.'

'They?'

'Yeah, *them*.' Rob let out a laugh. 'Those who know everything, or at least they claim to.'

'I'm not following.'

'Forget it. The point is, I was hoping you could do some drawings for my book. Illustrate it, maybe.'

'Sure. I'd love to.'

'Great. I'll show you the story when it's done.'

'Sounds good.'

'I don't want to tell you too much until I've finished, but you'll have total control over the drawings. That's your thing and I trust you with it.'

'Thanks. I appreciate that.'

'No problem.'

They stared at one another.

'Do you remember that day you nearly drowned?'

Alex nodded. 'Yeah.'

'It scared the shit out of me.'

'Me too.'

'I'd save you again if I had to — anytime, anywhere.'

'I know.'

There was another pause.

'I'll put Mum back on, okay? Make sure you keep writing.'

'Sure. Come see me again soon.'

'All right. Take care.' Alex handed his mother the receiver, his heart clenching tight.

Eight Mile Beach: A Memory

Rob stood upon the sand dunes, watching Alex approach the shoreline. His little brother reached the ocean's edge and fitted the goggles their mother had recently bought. The sound of a bird calling pierced the quiet, and Rob turned towards the sky to see two eagles hovering above. When he looked back towards the shore, his brother was wading into the water. He considered joining him, then decided against it.

Lying back on the sand, Rob watched the birds. They soared and dipped, mirroring each other's movements. He closed his eyes and listened to the steady hum of the ocean.

A small voice drifted towards him. He sat up and saw Alex drifting away from shore, his hand raised. Rob ran down the dunes and dove into the water. He resurfaced through breaking waves and swam hard. He stopped and scanned the water, but saw no sign of his brother.

Rob duck-dived and cold currents rushed against his face. His eyes stung. There was a pale mass further down, sinking almost beyond reach. The muscles in his legs pulled tight as he kicked hard, heading deeper.

Red swirls tainted the water. He touched something — fingers, a hand, a wrist. Grabbing hold, he turned and headed skyward. A yellow circle floated above, its edges diffused and glowing. His lungs burned and bright spots speckled his vision. He reached the surface, gasping for air and tasting blood. When his brother's face appeared, he saw that it had turned white.

Rob supported Alex with one arm and pulled him towards land with the other. Ahead of them, the ocean lifted, hiding the shoreline. His legs cramped, but he kept going. An eagle's cry caught his attention, taking his mind off the pain. He looked up and recognized the same birds he'd seen earlier; their talons were interlocked as they spiraled towards the water. Releasing one another moments before smashing into the sea, they darted in opposite directions.

A wave carried them into knee-deep water. Rob clasped Alex beneath the shoulders and dragged him onto the beach. He dropped to his knees and breathed into his brother's mouth.

Alex's chest rose and fell.

Rob pushed more air into his little brother.

Alex coughed, rolled onto his side and expelled water.

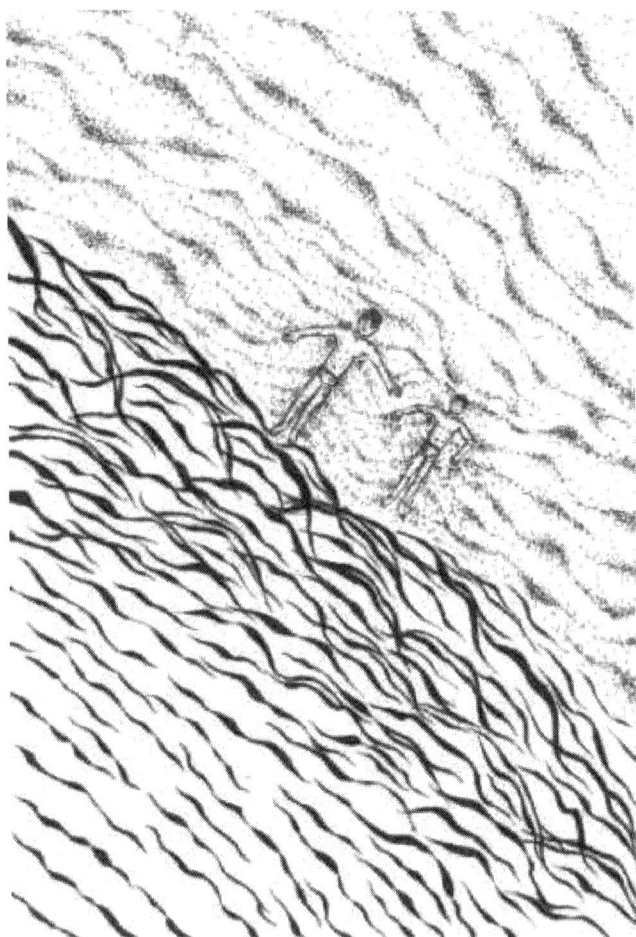

Resting on his haunches, Rob wiped his face and realized his nose was bleeding. Alex looked up at him.

They stared at one another, not saying a word.

Rob fell back onto the sand and closed his eyes. The earth felt warm and solid beneath him.

'Guess it's not time for me to die,' Alex said.

'Nope.'

Somewhere an eagle cried.

'Thanks for saving me anyway '

Rob turned to look at his little brother. 'Don't be thanking me — I plan to kick your arse as soon as we get up.'

'I know.'

High above, the eagles came back into view, soaring side by side as they headed to shore.

COMING FROM
MOONSHINE COVE IN 2018

FROM AUTHOR
EILEEN HERBERT-GOODALL

SISTER, LOVER, KEEPER

READ CHAPTER ONE
BEGINNING ON THE NEXT
PAGE

November 1909

Lizzie slept as I eased myself out of a chair, struck a match and lit the wick of a kerosene lamp beside her bed. Breathing in the fuel's pungent smell, I placed the flue into position and adjusted the flame. The darkness retreated a little, nightfall had come swiftly, catching me off guard. The days were growing short and ice-cold winds would soon blow in from the Celtic Sea. Perhaps they'd even travel up from the Great Southern Land, a place with which I'd become fascinated since reading of Shackleton's brazen adventures. I'd drawn the conclusion that his recent attempt to reach the South Pole had a certain neurosis about it. What else would drive a man to travel to the ends of the earth for a second time?

Standing by the window, I watched as the lighthouse of Bluff's Point maintained its steady rhythm, sweeping a golden beam across the black sea, back towards me, then away again. I never tired of observing the light, nor of performing my role as keeper, a position I'd acquired at the age of sixteen upon my father's death two years earlier. Since then, I'd fulfilled all duties associated with the lighthouse, even though they'd been officially passed down to my mother, who busied herself with other tasks such as tending our vegetable garden, looking after the chickens, and preparing meals. The authorities seemed content to let us be, with good reason — I was a well-trained keeper. Father had taken me to the lighthouse every day from the time I was five years old, until the day he died. He shared his knowledge in relation to preparing and maintaining the light, while also educating me about the importance of maintaining an accurate logbook. He instructed me in the use of Morse code, so I was able to operate the telegraph, and taught me to adeptly maneuver our row boat in the event that we might need to conduct a sea rescue. Most importantly, he made me aware of the grave responsibility associated with my role: there were lives at stake and one needed to stay alert.

As keeper, my chores began before dawn and continued well into the night. Firstly, I cleaned the Fresnel lens and its many prisms, then looked over the lamp before checking its fuel supply. Next came the trimming and lighting of the wick. Several times a day, the light's clockwork mechanism had to be unlocked and hand-cranked. This allowed weights to drop down the tower shaft and drive the gears that caused the lens to revolve. Given I needed to rise around midnight to again wind the clockwork, I chose to sleep in the lighthouse. Each evening, I would set my *Big Ben* alarm clock — a charming and truly modern invention with luminous hands —

but invariably woke a minute or two before the alarm rang. I suppose I'd become attuned to the light's rhythm.

Constructed in 1818, the lighthouse stood eighty feet tall and was painted entirely white, except for the exterior of the service room and the tower's dome, both of which were black. Sound construction and regular maintenance had kept the lighthouse and its surrounding buildings in good condition, although its history was steeped in drama and intrigue. The light's original keepers —twin brothers known as the McIvor boys — were aged just twenty-two when they first assumed their posts. They tended the light for fifty years, until disappearing in 1868. The crew of a supply ship discovered the brothers' absence after sending a dinghy ashore. Two crew members went in search of answers, but found none: there was no sign of the McIvors.

For years afterwards, people speculated about the keepers' fate. The case was purported to be a murder-suicide, with one brother having lost his mind, or an accidental double drowning. Some claimed the lighthouse was haunted by malicious spirits who caused the men to kill one another. As was the case with my father's death, no one knew the truth and circumstances surrounding the brothers' disappearance remained a mystery.

A few weeks after the McIvor boys vanished, the sole applicant for the position of lighthouse keeper, my grandfather, accepted his appointment at Bluff's Point. Douglas Wilson had worked as a lumberjack for two decades and was ready to strike out in a new direction. He and his wife, Maria, took what few possessions they owned, as well as their only child, three-year-old Christopher, and moved to the rugged coastline of southwest England. By all accounts, they shared a happy life at the lighthouse, until death intervened fifteen years later. My grandmother passed first, succumbing to Tuberculosis. Douglas died in his sleep two months later, supposedly of a broken heart. Just eighteen years old at the time, Christopher — my father — was determined to fulfill the responsibilities he'd inherited. He remained at the lighthouse along with a young, government-appointed assistant by the name of Patrick Hannan. When he was twenty-three, Christopher met his future wife, Margaret Robertson, at a dance in Abbotsville. He and my mother married in the summer of 1889. I was born a year later. Not long after, in early 1892, I received a sister. Around this time, having decided my family was entitled to its privacy, the authorities transferred Patrick Hannan to a different location.

I returned my attention to Lizzie, who stirred and muttered something. She opened her eyes as I pushed several strands of hair back from her face.

'It's all right,' I said. 'It's only me.'

'I know who you are,' Lizzie answered. 'I may be ill, but I've not lost my senses.'

'You were dreaming.'

The corners of Lizzie's mouth lifted. 'A wicked dream it was, too.'

I helped her into a sitting position. 'About what, dare I ask?'

'I dreamt you were kissing Daniel Lewis, right here in this very room.'

'You always did have a vivid imagination,' I said, fluffing up the blanket around her waist.

'I'm not imagining anything. The doctor fancies you, Ada.'

'Don't be daft.'

'I'm not daft,' Lizzie coughed before continuing, 'simply observant.'

'I've no time to indulge in silly fantasies. Besides, Daniel is merely doing his job. He wants you to get well — we all do.' I poured a glass of water from a jug on the bedside table and handed it to her. 'Drink this.'

Lizzie took a sip, then placed down the glass. Her hand shook as she did so, but I refrained from commenting; she needed no reminding of her fragility.

I walked to a serving table near the door, lifted a tray holding a bowl of warm soup and crossed the room once more. 'You must eat if you're to regain your strength.' I placed the tray on her lap.

'Yes,' she answered. 'I'll try.'

As I moved towards the window, a shaft of light ploughed through the darkness. In my mind's eye, I envisaged strange-looking cogs and wheels that maintained their perpetual rhythm deep within the lighthouse. I enjoyed sleeping in the tower and took solace in the knowledge that its internal workings were keeping others safe. In any case, my mother and sister weren't far — I only had to walk from the bottom of the lighthouse and through the storage room before reaching the kitchen located at the cottages' ocean end. All sections were connected under the same roof and there was no need to venture outside, although I often chose to. I'd been suffering from insomnia since my father's passing and had mentioned the matter to Daniel, hoping to gain his professional advice. He said my night-time wanderings indicated I was continuing to process the trauma associated with my father's death, an assertion I knew to be true. Still, I declined his offer of laudanum, which he regularly prescribed for Lizzie. As keeper, I couldn't afford such a luxury — heaven forbid that I should sleep through the night. Daniel also advised me to imagine myself somewhere safe and comfortable, until I felt at ease. I tried this practice on several occasions and subsequently heard strange voices that seemingly travelled upon the winds and waves. I was never frightened by such sounds; instead, I took comfort in the idea that nearby souls were helping me watch over the sea and those upon it. If nothing else, this notion kept loneliness at bay, as did the conversations I shared with Daniel.

In the short time we'd known each other, Daniel and I had discussed all manner of things: notions of happiness, our mutual desire to travel, the possibility of an afterlife, and even the sting of grief, with which he, too, was well acquainted. A few years earlier, while living in his hometown of London, Daniel had buried his wife and baby daughter, both of whom died during child birth. He was thirty years old when the tragedy struck. Escaping the city, he worked as a locomotive doctor before settling in Abbotsville. Daniel swiftly gained the respect and trust of his new patients. Yet, I harbored a nagging doubt concerning his ability to heal my sister: I feared that whatever ailed her might defy the most sophisticated medical treatment. I suppose such an outlook could be construed as pessimistic, but I would rather accept the harshness of truth, than cling to false hope.

Turning away from the window, I saw Lizzie attempting to place the tray upon the bedside table. I reached out and took it, noting she'd barely touched her soup.

'Thank you,' she said.

I acknowledged her gratitude with a dismissive wave.

'You take such good care of me, Ada.'

I smiled. 'Rest now. Daniel expects your condition to have improved when he returns tomorrow, and we wouldn't want to disappoint him.'

She gave me a mischievous wink. 'Of course not.'

Rolling my eyes, I carried the tray from the room.

That night in my dream, I walked along the rugged coastline, as I'd done countless times in the waking world. Dull hues surrounded me: the sea was grey, the sky dark, and steel-colored pebbles covered the beach. I turned towards the forest that stretched between Bluff's point and Abbotsville to see Daniel standing before the trees. He raised a hand, fingers silhouetted against the afternoon sunlight, then let it fall by his side. I pulled my coat in tight around my waist and stepped forward. When I reached him, neither of us spoke. He turned and headed into the woods. I followed in silence, sensing we were connected in ways I couldn't fathom.

A fog had descended and I caught only glimpses of Daniel as he made his way through the dense foliage. Birds called from the treetops, while the distant ocean hummed. I hurried on as thick bracken snatched at the hem of my skirt. Weaving my way through towering conifers, I reached a clearing and stepped into the sunshine.

All around, leaves shone yellow.

Daniel held my gaze as I approached, then stretched out his hand, revealing a small vile of clear liquid. I took it and held it up to the light, noting that gold flecks floated within it like tiny stars. I stared, enthralled. In my grasp, I understood, was the essence of hope.

We remained still, seemingly anchored in time, until a deep rumble erupted from the earth. The ground shook and between us a gaping chasm appeared before I slipped into the darkness. As I fell, I saw Daniel's face framed by a canvas of sky-blue. I knew he was screaming my name, although I heard only the relentless thumping of my pulse. The air was thick with dust and I struggled to breathe while tumbling through space.

A distant voice threatened to drag me back from the blackness, but I was reluctant to heed its call. I sensed there was no such thing as pain in the place waiting below. Rather, it seemed to offer the opportunity to drift on through a silent, unresponsive universe, with no one to love or lose. Such an arrangement would have suited me fine.

I opened my eyes to find myself seated in the wicker chair beneath Lizzie's bedroom window. The kerosene lamp glowed in the darkness. Daniel stood nearby, watching me. I attempted to speak, but coughed instead; my throat was bone-dry.

Daniel rested a hand on my shoulder. 'It sounded like you were having a bad dream.'

'Yes,' I answered.

'Are you alright?'

'Fine, thank you.'

'I've come to see how Elizabeth's faring.'

I looked at Lizzie sleeping in bed. 'What time is it?'

'Just after eight.'

'Please,' I said, 'have a seat.'

He took a chair from near the dressing table, placed it beside me, and sat down. 'How has she been?'

'Much the same. Early this morning she woke with a fever, but it passed not long after I gave her a dose of laudanum.'

He gestured towards a brown bottle on the bedside table. 'I've brought more.'

'Thank you.'

'I meant to get here earlier, but had to make an unexpected house call.'

'Nothing serious, I hope.'

'No.' He smiled. 'Jenny Powell is now the proud mother of a baby girl.'

'That's wonderful news. What's her name?'

'Charlotte.'

'How lovely. And all is well?'

'Yes, all is well.' He continued speaking in a soft voice: 'It may not be the best time, but I wish to talk with you about Elizabeth.'

'What is it?'

'I'm concerned.'

My gaze drifted to the window. Outside a beam of light cut through the night, vanished, then reappeared moments later.

'She fell ill more than two months ago and should be showing signs of recovery.'

I gave no response.

'There may be an underlying cause behind the pleurisy, perhaps a growth inside the lungs fanning the inflammation.'

'What are you saying, Daniel?'

'I suspect her condition will continue to deteriorate.'

'But you can't be certain?'

'No.'

'And time will tell?'

'I believe so.'

'What are we talking about? Weeks? Months?'

'I don't know.'

I glanced at Lizzie; her eyes remained shut and her breathing sounded shallow.

'I hope I'm wrong, Ada.'

I kept quiet. What was there to say?

An owl's call broke the silence. I frequently spotted the birds when I walked about at night, but could never be sure if they regarded me as friend or foe — the expression behind their eyes was indiscernible.

'Have you told my mother?' I asked.

'No.'

'Good, don't mention anything. Not until we're sure of the prognosis.'

'Of course.'

I stared at the lamp, which spilt a golden hue across the floor. 'Thank you.'

The owl cried out again and I couldn't help but wonder if it were warning me of things yet to come.

Printed in Australia
AUOC02n1642170317
283966AU00002B/2/P

9 781945 181078